W9-CBF-512

THE
MYSTERY OF THE
MARTELLO TOWER

THE
MYSTERY OF THE
MARTELLO
TOWER

Jennifer Lanthier

LAURA GERINGER BOOKS
An Imprint of HarperCollins*Publishers*

For Jane and Jim Lanthier

The Mystery of the Martello Tower
Copyright © 2006 by Jennifer Lanthier
All rights reserved. Printed in the United States of America.
No part of this book may be used or reproduced in any manner whatsoever without written permission except in the case of brief quotations embodied in critical articles and reviews. For information address HarperCollins Children's Books, a division of HarperCollins Publishers, 1350 Avenue of the Americas, New York, NY 10019.
www.harpercollinschildrens.com

Library of Congress Cataloging-in-Publication Data
Lanthier, Jennifer.
    The mystery of the Martello tower / by Jennifer Lanthier. — 1st U.S. ed.
        p. cm.
    "Originally published in Canada by HarperTrophyCanada, an imprint of HarperCollins Publishers Ltd., in 2006."
    Summary: In their attempts to solve the mystery of their father's disappearance, Hazel and her brother, Ned, find themselves involved with a trio of art thieves and uncover some disturbing family secrets.
    ISBN 978-0-06-125712-4 (trade bdg.)
    ISBN 978-0-06-125713-1 (lib. bdg.)
    [1. Art thefts—Fiction. 2. Brothers and sisters—Fiction. 3. Fathers—Fiction. 4. Family problems—Fiction. 5. Mystery and detective stories. 6. Canada—Fiction.] I. Title.
PZ7.L2918Mys 2008   2007021356
[Fic]—dc22 CIP
                                                        AC

Typography by Carla Weise
1 2 3 4 5 6 7 8 9 10
❖
First U.S. Edition
Originally published in Canada by HarperTrophyCanada, an imprint of HarperCollins Publishers Ltd., in 2006.

PROLOGUE

Hazel Frump tried to cry out, but her voice had disappeared. Get up, get up, *get up,* she urged herself.

But she could only lie still, listening to the ragged sound of her own breathing. The stone of the flagged floor in the old tower room was cool and rough beneath her cheek, faintly illuminated by the stars shining through the tall, arched windows. This was crazy. She had to get out of here before they found her.

Hazel stared at her legs, willing them to move. Nothing. If only she could crawl to that window, maybe she could climb out and escape. Why couldn't she move?

What am I doing here? she cried silently. No, that was the wrong question.

What am I doing here *again*?

1

"**H**azel!"

Hazel awoke with a jolt, certain she had heard her father call her name. She opened her eyes and instantly snapped them shut again. The light streaming through her windows was strong enough to blind her. Where was she? And what time was it?

With one hand shading her face, Hazel squinted cautiously around the room. It *was* her room, she noted with relief. She was back at home, in the apartment in the city; not in her dormitory at boarding school, and definitely not captive in some musty old tower.

She could see her posters of basketball players and the ball autographed by Rafer Alston, who had made it all the way from the Rucker playground to the

NBA. Next to it was her computer, with its basketball screen saver. Against the far wall was the hoop set to NCAA height, and a few feet away was the window she'd cracked last night when she'd failed to grab a rebound. It was her room, all right.

"Hazel! Helloooo? Hazel? Earth calling Hazel!"

A small boy with ruler-straight brown hair stood at the side of her bed, polishing his glasses. Now that he finally had her attention, he placed the spectacles on his nose and peered anxiously at her.

"You were having that dream again," he said. "Weren't you?"

Hazel glared at her brother. She was sweating; her thick hair was plastered to her neck and her forehead felt clammy. Her skin was flushed as red as her hair, and she was tangled up in her quilt.

"What are you doing in my room?" she asked, ignoring Ned's question.

"Have you ever noticed that every time you have that dream, something bad happens?"

Hazel groaned. Why had she ever told Ned about the dream? She'd done it in a moment of weakness after trying to talk to their father about it. A strange look had appeared in Colin Frump's eyes, and he had quickly changed the subject.

"I think if you ask around, you'll find that *most* people associate nightmares with bad things happening," Hazel replied. "It's called stress, Squirt."

"Actually, I think if *you* ask around, you'll find that *most* people have nightmares *after* something bad happens. You have them *before*," Ned said, mimicking her tone. "Specifically, you have this one dream. And then something bad happens."

Hazel slumped against the pillows. Ned at nine and a half was widely regarded as brilliant; they had so little in common, they practically spoke a different language. They didn't look much alike either. It wasn't just their hair. About to turn twelve, Hazel was as tall for her age as Ned was short for his. Her eyes were green; his were brown. And while her skin was the color of milk, Ned looked tanned all year long.

"Ned, nothing bad is going to happen," Hazel insisted. Ned raised one eyebrow. He did it because he knew it drove her crazy. Their father could raise one eyebrow too. But try as she might, Hazel could only raise both eyebrows. It was frustrating being the only one who couldn't do it. She suspected her mother hadn't been able to do it either, but Jane Frump had died before Hazel's fourth birthday, and Hazel couldn't remember much about her. She didn't like to ask their father—he always looked so sad whenever her mother's name was mentioned.

"Look, it's the first day of summer vacation . . . school is, like, a hundred miles away, and by the smell of things, I'd say Dad is cooking bacon and eggs for a welcome-home breakfast." Hazel kicked at her covers. She had managed to get one leg free, but the other had a sheet wound around it so tightly, it was a miracle her circulation wasn't cut off. "Except for me being attacked by killer sheets, there's nothing bad here," she said. "I'll bet you a month's allowance."

"You can pay me anytime," Ned answered. His voice sounded odd, as if his throat had tightened. "Frankie's the one in the kitchen, and if you actually want to be able to *eat* the bacon, you better get out there and take over," he said.

Hazel was stunned. "*Frankie's* in the kitchen?"

Frankie couldn't cook. She lived in the loft just across the hall and helped their father run his art gallery. But she *never* helped him cook.

"Where's Dad?" asked Hazel.

"Gone," answered Ned.

Gone?

Ned put his head down and turned away. Hazel could see he was, once again, obsessively polishing his spotless glasses.

"All I can tell you, honey, is that he called me late last night and said something important had come up and he had to catch an overseas flight early this morning," said Frankie. "He was supposed to knock on my door before he called the taxi, but he must have been running late, because by the time I opened my door, he was getting in the elevator. He seemed pretty stressed—when I called his name, he almost dropped one of the paintings he was carrying."

Frankie slid a plate of charred meat and leathery eggs over to Hazel. "I can't understand why my cooking never looks the same as other people's," she said, frowning.

Ned poured the remains of a box of cereal into a bowl.

"I'm not really hungry," Hazel said, trying to avoid looking at the eggs. "Where *exactly* did Dad say he was going, and when did he say he'd be back?"

"Well, he didn't, dear, that's the thing," Frankie answered, throwing her hands in the air in a gesture the children knew well. "I'm assuming he'll be back in time for your birthday. You know your father. Colin Frump is not a chatty man."

"Yes, but he's not . . . I mean, he's not the sort of person who just goes running off into the night—"

"Or the morning," Ned interrupted.

"—without an explanation," Hazel continued. "He's not . . ."

"Impulsive," Ned finished her thought.

"Yeah," Hazel agreed. "He's . . ."

"Secretive," said Ned.

"I was going to say *cautious*," Hazel corrected him. "But yeah, I guess you could say he's . . . guarded. Reserved. The sort of person who studies all the angles before he makes a move."

"Well, right now he's the sort of person who's left *me* responsible for keeping his gallery open *and* calling all his clients to cancel his appointments *and* looking after you two—just when I'm trying to get my next show ready," Frankie said.

A twinge of guilt pricked at Hazel's conscience. It hadn't occurred to her that they might be messing up Frankie's life.

"Don't worry, Frankie. Ned and I don't need any looking after," Hazel said, trying to make her voice sound mature and reassuring.

"We can definitely take over the meals," Ned said, his mouth full of cereal.

"And we can help at the gallery, too," Hazel added, shooting her brother a warning glance.

"Oh, the gallery!" Frankie said. "I've got to get over there. Listen, would you kids mind awfully . . . no, I can't ask you that. You've just returned home, back to your own beds. . . ."

"Ask us what?" Hazel said.

"Well, I have lots of work to do to get ready for my show, and since I'm going to be in the gallery most of the day, I was thinking . . ."

"You were thinking if we slept across the hall at your place instead of here, you could paint all night," Hazel guessed. She shrugged and glanced at Ned.

"We don't mind," Ned said, "so long as we can use our rooms during the day."

Frankie nodded. Hazel and Ned had grown up treating Frankie's apartment like an extension of their own. When their father had renovated the warehouse, he had created only two apartments on each floor. The elevator wouldn't stop at any floor unless you had the right key. And since no one but Frankie and the Frumps had keys to their floor, they hardly ever locked either door during the day. When they were younger, Colin Frump had tried to discourage his children from wandering in and out of Frankie's apartment, afraid they might disturb her work. But Frankie had never objected. Besides, if Frankie was in the middle of painting, you could walk in with a wheelbarrow and walk out with everything she owned, except for her paints and brushes, and she would never notice.

"That's settled then," Frankie said, sounding relieved. "I'll go open the gallery. Why don't you two drop by around lunchtime and we can all go to Café Gentil?"

Ned looked at the clock. It was already noon. He looked at Hazel.

"It sounds like you have a lot to do at the gallery,"

she said. "What if Ned and I come by around closing, and we'll have dinner at the café?"

"Sure, sweetie," Frankie agreed. "Whatever you say."

"Great," Ned said. "Now if you'll excuse me, I've got to go email my chemistry club."

"I didn't know nine-year-olds did chemistry," Frankie marveled as Ned padded down the hall toward his room. "Although I suppose he will be ten soon. . . ."

"Even twelve-year-olds don't do chemistry," Hazel told her. "But Ned's started doing a lot of stuff online this year. I'll bet the other members of this club don't have a clue who they're dealing with—they probably think he's twenty-one or something."

Frankie nodded thoughtfully. "It can't be easy always being the smartest one in the room, especially at his age."

"Hey! Standing right here, Frankie," Hazel said.

"Oh, sweetheart, you're smart too," Frankie said soothingly. "But you know what I mean."

Hazel rolled her eyes. But she did know what Frankie meant.

Hazel waited until she heard the door close behind Frankie before making her way to the garbage can to dump the cold, alien substance that had congealed on her plate. Her father always said coffee was the only thing you could trust Frankie to make in the kitchen, because she'd learned to make the sweet, rich brew when she was a student in Turkey. But Hazel had always wondered why Frankie hadn't picked up any cooking tips when she'd lived in Italy or France.

The eggs sounded oddly heavy as they landed at the bottom of the pail.

"Hazel!"

Hazel jumped, dropping her plate in the sink.

Frankie was standing in the doorway.

"Whoa, Frankie, you startled me," said Hazel, moving away from the garbage can.

"I did? Oh, honey, maybe it's really not such a good idea—you guys hanging out here on your own. You seem nervous."

"No, I'm fine," Hazel replied. "Uh, did you need something?"

"I just forgot to tell you that your dad mentioned he would try to email you, so you should check your computer later."

"Okay. Does he have his cell phone with him?"

"Umm . . . I think so. But he warned me he wouldn't have it on very much. Anyway, I'm sure he'll be in touch soon. See you later!"

This time Hazel saw Frankie to the door and watched as she entered the elevator.

After she had gone, the apartment seemed very

quiet. Hazel stood for a moment, listening to the distant sounds of plumbing upstairs and traffic in the street below. She couldn't have said why, exactly, but when she closed the sturdy oak door, she bolted it behind her.

The afternoon crawled by more slowly than a math class on a warm September afternoon. Hazel tried dialing her father's cell phone once, just to see what would happen. A recorded voice told her the customer was "not in the service area."

After showering, dressing, and checking her computer for email about two hundred times, Hazel decided she needed some fresh air. Grabbing a basketball from the stash in her closet, she dribbled it down the hall toward Ned's room.

"Hey, Squirt—let's hit the court and you can show me how much you've improved since last fall," Hazel called.

Ned stuck his head out the door.

"If you promise not to call me that, I *might* go one-on-one before we meet Frankie," he told her. "But I'm in the middle of something right now."

The door slammed behind him.

Last summer, Ned had pestered her constantly to shoot hoops. She knew how hard he'd been working on his shot during the school year. She'd assumed he would be eager to show off.

I bet this has something to do with my birthday next week, Hazel told herself as she headed back to her room.

Ned always gave her a present he'd made himself. This wasn't as lame as it sounded, since Ned was not only a genius but also good with his hands. Still, his idea of what constituted a fun gift didn't always match Hazel's—like the time he designed glow-in-the-dark remote-controlled spiders with realistic hairy legs. "Surrealistic hairy legs," their dad had called them, after one of the spiders crawled into the shower with him.

Thinking about her father was giving Hazel a headache. Her mind was going in circles, chasing the same questions over and over.

Why had he left in such a hurry? Where *was* he? What was he doing? Today was Wednesday. Had he even remembered that next Wednesday was her birthday? Would he make it back in time? Did he even care? What could be so important that he would take off without telling them?

Hazel could feel her pulse jumping as she turned on her heel and tiptoed back past Ned's door. She didn't want to have to explain her plan. For as long as she could remember, Hazel and Ned had never been allowed into their dad's study. They were never sure what he did there, but when it came to their father, they weren't sure about much. Hazel hated to admit it, but Ned was right—Dad was secretive. He had no family except them and never spoke of his childhood. He never spoke of their mother, either, claiming both subjects were too painful. All they knew was that Jane Frump had died when Hazel was not quite four and Ned was a baby.

Hazel had figured out a few things about her father over the years. One was that he was rich and generous. Ned believed he was one of the richest men in Canada. Hazel figured that was an exaggeration, but he was wealthy enough not to have a job. The gallery Frankie was running was just one of Colin Frump's hobbies, like the building where they lived. Hazel knew from talking to the tenants that her father didn't charge enough rent to cover the costs of maintaining the building. Some of them didn't pay rent at all.

Yet whenever she asked him about it, he made a shooing gesture. Then he'd start asking about her grades in math class.

Yes, her father was a mystery. Maybe all fathers were something of a mystery, but hers was more so. Over the years she had come up with tons of questions she knew there was no point in asking—her father would never answer. There were big questions, obvious ones, such as: Where did he come from? Where did he get all his money? What was Jane Frump like?

Was Hazel at all like her? Why wouldn't he ever talk about her? What were his parents like? Then there were the littler questions: Why didn't he really have any friends? Why did he always seem to be someplace else, even when Hazel was hugging him and telling him how happy she was to be home for the holidays? Why was that someplace else so far away and so . . . *sad?*

Years ago, Hazel and her father had climbed to the lookout at Pirate's Peak. She hadn't felt the least bit afraid as they peered over the edge, down to the valley far below. Not until her father had remarked, "You know, they say the fear is not that you will *fall,* but that you will *jump.*" Ever since that moment, Hazel had been a little worried about her father. And about heights.

Hazel hesitated before the door to her father's study. She almost hoped it would be locked. Once she entered, there'd be no going back. And what if she found some kind of explanation for Colin Frump's wealth that was embarrassing or . . . illegal?

But what if she found something about her mother?

Hazel had never even seen a photograph of Jane Frump. There were no pictures in the apartment of her mother. No pictures of her father's family either. There had been a fire years ago, her father said. A terrible fire. He refused to say anything more.

Still, Hazel had always hoped for her father's sake that *something* had survived the fire. It was too sad to think of her dad having nothing but memories. She imagined a single, badly singed photograph of her mother, tucked carefully into a desk drawer. Or maybe a bundle of letters—or a diary.

The brass handle turned easily, and the heavy oak door swung open.

Like the rest of the loft, the room was furnished sparingly, with stark modern furniture and messy stacks of books. The only difference was that in the rest of the apartment, just a few meticulously chosen paintings were hung with care. Here there were hundreds of paintings, from oil canvases to watercolors. They covered the room from floor to ceiling. Framed or unframed, they were leaning against bookshelves, heaped atop the sofa, and piled on chairs. In the center of the room lay a stack of canvases, wrapped in brown paper, ready to be mailed.

There had to be a desk hidden somewhere in the clutter. Hazel spied a long folding screen at the far end of the room.

Carefully, she made her way past a precariously balanced canvas almost twice her height and narrowly avoided tripping over the group of marble statues it concealed. The area behind the screen was almost as cluttered, but here the mess consisted of notebooks, letters, and files piled on the floor and strewn across a broad antique desk. Jutting out like islands in the sea of paper were computer monitors, hard drives, two printers, and a telephone.

Hazel sat down gingerly. She noticed a small notepad to the left of the telephone. Her father was clearly in the habit of doodling while he talked. She flipped through the three pages remaining on the pad. They were filled with scribbles—words and drawings.

"Time for a new pad, Dad," Hazel muttered. She stuck the sheets into her pocket to decipher later. Her father had left the computer running. It took only moments to find his email account. There were two unread messages. The first was from someone named Oliver Frump. The subject heading read: "Frump Family Reunion on Île du Loup?"

Family reunion? But Colin Frump had no family. Hazel's finger hovered over the computer mouse, ready to click and open the message. Then her eye focused on the second unread message.

It was from someone named Inspector O'Toole.

Hazel froze.

The subject of this message read: "Interpol investigation into Ned's website."

2

Hazel stared at the computer screen.

Interpol—that was some sort of international police thing, wasn't it? What did they investigate? Crime, obviously. But what sort of crime? Hazel felt stupid. Ned would know, of course. But she couldn't ask him.

Why would Interpol be investigating her little brother? What had Ned done?

She caught her breath. Was he *really* designing a bomb with that chemistry club? Ned wasn't that clever, was he? She shook her head; wrong question.

Ned wasn't that *stupid*, was he?

Hazel had thought her brain was stuffed so full of worry and questions about her father that there was no room for anything else. But her head seemed to be expanding like a balloon, swelling with fresh questions every minute. Was this why her dad had left the country? Was he protecting Ned somehow?

But if Ned was in trouble, shouldn't Colin Frump be here?

Hazel's brain felt dangerously close to popping. How could the police—the *international* police—be investigating Ned?

"He's just a little kid," Hazel thought aloud.

Maybe it wasn't a bomb. Maybe it was something to do with hacking, or designing viruses to mess up other people's computers. She'd read an article about that stuff for school. It seemed to be something smart kids—often boys—got into just because they could. Like a way of showing off.

Maybe that was all it was.

Except hackers could go to jail. What if Ned had hacked into the computer system of a hospital and somebody had open-heart surgery instead of getting his tonsils taken out? What if he had hacked into a server that controlled traffic and gave everyone green lights so that they all drove into each other? What if he'd made the navy think a fishing boat was a submarine—and they blew it up?

Hazel closed her eyes against the images that crowded her brain. Ned was a pest, but he was not a criminal.

It had to be something else.

There was only one way to find out. She had to open her father's emails.

Yet as her fingers hovered over the keys, Hazel hesitated. What would her dad say when he found out she'd read his messages? Wouldn't he know someone had seen them?

Hazel wished she'd paid more attention when Ned talked about computers. There was probably something she could do, some way to make the computer think she hadn't read the messages.

Ned would know.

Hazel pulled at her hair. She would just have to open the messages and hope for the best. Maybe their father would understand. It's not like she had *wanted* to go snooping around—he'd left her no choice. If her dad had taken the time to talk to her before leaving, if he had called from the airport or emailed from his hotel . . .

Hazel slumped back in the chair. She could hear a faint tapping noise in the distance; Claire Holland must be sculpting again.

Maybe it would be best to check her own computer one more time before she did anything rash. Maybe she'd find an email from Colin Frump explaining everything. But even if her father came clean about this whole Interpol thing, there was still the question of that Oliver Frump guy and his family reunion. Finding long-lost family you never knew you had wasn't as important as figuring out why the cops were after your kid brother, but it was still worth looking into.

Once again, her fingers moved toward the keyboard.

The faint tapping noise became a loud thumping. That wasn't Claire Holland sculpting upstairs. That was someone banging on the apartment door.

"Hazel? Ned? It's me. Open up!"

Hazel jumped to her feet. What was Frankie doing back already? She glanced at her watch. How time flies when your world is falling apart. It was almost dinnertime. Frankie must have decided not to wait for them. Hazel picked her way through the study as quickly as she could, without toppling anything over.

Ned was still in his room. Hazel could hear him tapping away at his keyboard as she ran to open the apartment door. He really wouldn't notice if the place burned down around him, Hazel reflected.

"Hey, Hazel—I hope you guys don't mind takeout instead of the café." Frankie smiled and handed Hazel a shopping bag filled with cartons of Chinese food. "Should we eat here or over at my place?"

"Oh. Uh, let's eat here," Hazel answered. She was pleased to find her voice sounded calm.

"Where's Ned?" Frankie asked.

"He's in his room. I'll set the table if you can get him out," Hazel offered. "I've been trying—I think the hard drive ate him or something."

"So, you slept all morning and stayed inside all afternoon?" Frankie said. "What a shame—it was so sunny out."

While Frankie went to rouse Ned, Hazel placed bamboo mats on the Lucite dining table and set chopsticks at each place. Normal, normal, normal, she repeated silently to herself. I must act *normal*.

As she poured glasses of ice water for everyone, Hazel resolved to check her computer after dinner, just one last time. If she had no email from her dad, she'd find a way to sneak back into the study and read his. It was that simple.

Except, of course, it wasn't simple at all.

After dinner Frankie insisted they all go for a stroll along the boardwalk, since the children had spent so much time "cooped up indoors." Ordinarily Hazel loved to walk with Frankie, who had a different way of looking at the world. She could always count on Frankie to point out faces and patterns or shadows that Hazel would never have noticed otherwise. But tonight Hazel was so anxious to get back to her father's study, she found herself nodding without hearing anything Frankie said.

Hazel felt sure Ned and Frankie must suspect

something every time they looked at her, but no one said a word. Maybe she was a better actress than she realized. Maybe they figured she was just sad about Colin Frump's leaving.

By the time they returned to the apartment, it was late and darkness had settled over the city. Frankie waited in the kitchen while the children gathered pajamas, toothbrushes, and a change of clothes for the morning. Hazel just had time to see that there were no messages from her father before Ned was calling to her to hurry up so they could go across the hall to Frankie's place.

As the pair settled themselves on futons in Frankie's guest room, Ned told Hazel that Frankie had made him promise not even to turn on his computer the next day. He and Hazel were supposed to spend the morning shooting hoops in the park, before meeting Frankie for lunch at Café Gentil.

Rats! thought Hazel.

Ned was quiet for a long time after Hazel turned out the light. When he finally spoke, it was in a whisper. "Do you think maybe this time the dream was wrong?" he asked. "Because nothing really terrible has happened. Yet."

Hazel was grateful for the darkness that hid her face. No, nothing terrible. Unless you counted that Interpol investigation and Dad's mysterious disappearance.

"That's what I've been telling you," she replied. "Frankie's here, I'm here. Everything's okay."

"Yeah." Ned sounded unconvinced. "But the dream's never been wrong before."

That was true. As Hazel searched for something reassuring to say, Ned asked the question he'd clearly been working up to, his voice tinged with dread.

"What if you have the dream again tonight?"

Hazel shivered. Please, don't let me have the dream again tonight.

"I won't," she said in the most confident tone she could muster.

It seemed to work, because when Ned spoke again, he sounded almost normal.

"I'm sorry I kept you in all day." Ned's apology was muffled by his pillow. "I didn't really think about the fact that you couldn't go out if I didn't—not until Frankie pointed it out just now."

"That's okay," Hazel said. "So, uh, did you get a lot done?"

"What do you mean?"

"You know—with your chemistry club. Everything go okay?

"I guess." Ned sounded suspicious.

Hazel decided to change the subject. "So, I've been meaning to ask you," she said. "This girl at school got into trouble for reading someone else's emails . . . and

I was thinking. Couldn't she have disguised the fact that she'd read them somehow?"

"It's wrong to read other people's emails," Ned said sleepily.

"Oh yeah, absolutely," Hazel said quickly. "But I just wondered why she didn't, you know, hide her tracks, or whatever. Because there's got to be something she could have done, right?"

Ned yawned. "Well, I think most systems have a way you can mark the emails as unread if you look in the toolbar—you know, the thing across the top of the computer screen," he said. "But she could also have just deleted the emails after she read them, and then the person who sent them would have thought they got lost in cyberspace. Things disappear on the Internet all the time."

Hazel could feel herself blush. Talk about stupid! Ned's solution was so simple, it was ridiculous. What was her science teacher always saying? The easiest solution is often the right one? She didn't need any complicated computer wizardry: If she couldn't figure out how to mark the messages as unread, she'd just destroy the evidence.

Hazel thought about doing it right then. She could make some excuse to Frankie about needing a book or something from the apartment. It wouldn't take long to read those two messages (and any others that might have come in since). She didn't have to worry about memorizing them or anything, because it wasn't like she had to delete them right away. She could even print paper copies!

So long as she erased them before Colin Frump's return, no one would be the wiser.

Hazel stifled a yawn. She really, *really* wanted to find out more about Inspector O'Toole and Interpol . . . not to mention this Oliver Frump guy. Sure, he might just be some distant relative, like a fifth cousin or something. But what if he actually knew something about her family? Maybe Oliver had met her dad before—maybe he'd even met her mom! There had to be some way Hazel could get ahold of Oliver without her father finding out. But it had been kind of an exhausting day. Her legs felt like weights.

Ned was already asleep—she could tell by his breathing. Hazel wasn't surprised. Frankie's futons were awfully comfortable.

"I'll check the emails tomorrow," she told herself.

It was a decision she would regret.

Breakfast at Frankie's wasn't too horrible. Hazel and Ned managed to convince her that cold cereal and fruit were just perfect, so no actual cooking was required. She made a great production of walking them to the park and actually watched them warm up for a few minutes before setting off for the gallery.

"She's serious about this fresh air thing," Ned said as he dribbled the ball up the empty court.

"You know, I really don't mind if you want to go back to the apartment," Hazel said. "We can shoot a few hoops before we go, so we don't have to lie to Frankie."

"Nope. I promised her I'd spend the day outdoors."

"Well, yeah, but . . . we could go home for a bit, and then come back and go one-on-one for an hour or so before we meet her for lunch."

"Why are you so eager to leave?" Ned asked. He had stopped dribbling the ball and was staring at her. "I thought you'd be dying to show me you're still better than I am." Hazel could feel a flush creeping over her pale skin. She hoped Ned would think it was the heat.

"I'm . . . I'm not," she stammered. "Not eager to leave, I mean. In fact, I plan to kick your—I mean, I'm taking you to school, Squirt. Right now. Bring it on."

"Anyone named Hazel can't say 'bring it on,'" Ned said. "Face it. You're just not that cool."

Hazel grabbed the ball from his hands and launched a perfect midrange jump shot. The ball arced through the air and dropped through the net without touching the hoop.

"Nice," Ned said. "But you should also lose the 'taking you to school' thing. Makes you sound like you're trying too hard to be a 'baller.' "

"What is this? Your version of trash talk?" Hazel asked. "Do you really think you can throw me off my game?"

She launched another jump shot, but this one clanged off the rim.

"Looks like it," Ned said.

That was enough to make Hazel set aside her worries about her father and Inspector O'Toole. For the next two hours they played Twenty-one and H-O-R-S-E, and competed against each other in countless drills they knew from school. It wasn't a fair contest. Hazel was tall and had played starting point guard on her school team ever since she began attending boarding school three years ago. Ned was short and had only joined a team this past year, after he became a boarder. Still, Hazel was quick to admit her brother had been working hard.

"You've really improved, Squirt. You've come a long way since the last time we played," she told him. They took a break in the shade of a leafy maple tree to swig Gatorade and catch their breath.

"Thanks," Ned said. "There's this kid at my school, William Cowan. He's been helping me with my layup. He's really good."

"Well, now you are too," Hazel said.

Ned wiped his mouth with his hand and peered at her, considering.

"Really?" he said after a moment. "Don't you want to add anything?"

Hazel thought for a second.

"You still need to work on your crossover and your left-handed dribble," she ventured.

"No, I meant, like, a joke. Usually if you say something nice to me, you say something funny and kind of mean afterward."

Hazel felt as if her face had just been slapped. "No I don't," she said. "Do I?"

"Not serious mean," Ned said. "Funny mean. It's like . . . it's sort of like you take back the compliment."

Hazel's stomach lurched. Maybe it was too much sports drink. On the other hand, maybe it was guilt. Because now that he'd said it, she could see that she did do that, all the time. Not just to Ned, either.

"I'm sorry, Ned," she said after a moment. "I didn't mean to hurt your feelings."

"It's okay, no big deal," said Ned.

He didn't look at Hazel as he spoke. He was too busy polishing his glasses with the edge of his T-shirt. Watching him, Hazel had the sensation of seeing him clearly for the first time. He was so much smaller than she, but he seemed . . . well, much older than she remembered.

"I wouldn't mind going home and grabbing a shower before we meet Frankie for lunch," Hazel suggested. "Do you think we have time?"

Ned looked at his watch.

"Nope," he said. "What is it with you and going home? We couldn't go even if there was time, anyway. I didn't bring my key."

"So? What's wrong with mine?"

"Hazel, you don't have your key! Didn't you notice Frankie borrowing it before she left?" Ned asked. "She took it from your knapsack. She said she might need to go back and pick up some papers from Dad's study."

"But Frankie has her own key to our place," Hazel said.

"She lost it," Ned said. He raised one eyebrow. "She told us last night when we were out on that walk, remember? She said she was sure she'd left it on her desk at the gallery yesterday, but when she went to leave, she couldn't find it anywhere."

"Oh. I guess I wasn't paying attention," Hazel confessed.

"No kidding," Ned said. "You were totally out of it last night."

"I didn't think you guys noticed," said Hazel. She stood up, stretching her right leg.

"I don't think *Frankie* noticed," Ned said. "She was too freaked out about losing the key, and trying to find some painting, and all those phone calls from some artist in New York that Dad was supposed to be meeting this week."

Hazel blinked. She really had been out of it last night. She had no memory of Frankie discussing any of this.

"You know, if you're done wiping the court with me, we should go to the gallery," Ned said. "Frankie could probably use our help."

Hazel nodded and stuffed the basketball and drinks into her bag.

The gallery was just two blocks away, on a street that ran north from the lake. It was a street that served as an unofficial dividing line between the leafy residential neighborhood to the east and the old warehouse district and dockyards to the west, which Colin Frump and a few other investors had turned into an artists' enclave. The gallery was housed in an old chocolate factory. Colin Frump had chosen it for its soaring ceilings and giant windows, but Hazel swore it was the lingering smell of chocolate that encouraged buyers.

The gallery was known for featuring artists who were young or just starting out, selling "art for people who can't afford art," as Frankie once said. So Ned and Hazel were taken aback to see a gleaming Ferrari convertible parked out front. Ned was so enthralled by the bright red car, he stopped dead in his tracks, a dazed expression on his face. Hazel didn't care much for cars, and was more interested in the fact that it was parked in front of a fire hydrant, underneath a sign that read: NO STOPPING ANYTIME. She glared at the driver, who was still behind the wheel.

"Some people just think they can do whatever they want," Hazel muttered. But Ned didn't seem to hear her.

"What if there was a fire?" she continued. "He'd probably let the gallery burn down before he'd move out of the way. Is he napping, or what?"

She was tempted to approach the bored-looking blond man as he reclined against the leather headrest, his tweed cap pulled low over his forehead and his eyes shaded by dark glasses. But the local parking cop, Officer Cohen, beat her to it.

"Sir, you're blocking a fire hydrant. I'll have to ask you to move."

Without looking up, the driver slipped his hand into his shirt pocket and produced a fifty-dollar bill, which he dangled over the side of the car.

Big mistake. Hazel smiled to herself. Officer Cohen would never accept so much as a cup of coffee for free. Ferrari Guy had just guaranteed himself a ticket.

It would be fun to watch, but they should be inside, helping Frankie.

"C'mon, Ned," she urged, tugging at his sleeve.

"I'll be there in a second. Just want to get a better look at the car," Ned said.

Hazel was sure he didn't even see the driver or Officer Cohen, just the sleek lines of the flame-red sports car.

"Whatever."

Hazel pushed open the glass door and noticed that the bell that was supposed to tinkle every time the door opened or closed made no sound. She was about to call out to Frankie to ask if she'd realized it was broken, when she heard a low, angry voice—a man's voice—from the back of the gallery. Then a woman cried out in pain.

It was Frankie.

"I told you I have no idea what you're talking about," Frankie cried. "Please—you're hurting my arm—let go!"

Hazel stood rooted to the spot.

She couldn't see who was hurting Frankie. Her view was blocked by a series of giant canvases staggered at intervals throughout the gallery. Was there more than one guy back there?

Hazel's mind was racing. If she couldn't see them, they couldn't see her. She drew a deep, steadying breath and called out to Frankie in as grown-up a voice as she could muster. "Ms. Yazer? Oh, Ms. Yazer! Is everything all right?"

Her voice trembled a little, but even to her own ears she sounded older. Hazel paused, but neither

Frankie nor the man replied. So far, so good. At least she'd startled the man into silence. Now, if she could just make him leave.

"It's Susan Cummings, Ms. Yazer," she continued, using the name of a girl at school. "I just came by to pick up that painting and I . . . uh . . . I noticed a police officer outside. I hope that man in the red convertible isn't one of your clients, dear. I think he's getting a ticket."

Hazel heard a muffled curse and the sound of heavy footsteps on the creaking floor. She just had time to duck behind a huge canvas covered in paint splotches. A heavyset man with a large bulbous nose and bald head lumbered toward the door. Peeking around a corner of the painting, Hazel saw a jagged scar on the man's neck. An enormous diamond ring flashed from one of his fleshy fingers. He was quite possibly the ugliest man Hazel had ever seen.

"I'll be back. You'd better have that painting," he flung over his shoulder as he pushed open the door.

Hazel ran to find Frankie.

She was sitting on an antique chesterfield, rubbing her left arm. She looked shaken, but when she saw Hazel, she tried to smile.

"Susan Cummings, I presume?" Frankie asked.

"It was the first name that popped into my head. Are you okay?" Hazel asked her. "Officer Cohen really is outside, you know. I'll go and get her."

"No!" Frankie's voice was abrupt. But she seemed to realize it almost at once and covered her mouth with her hand. She shook her head apologetically.

"Hazel, I'm sorry. I didn't mean to snap. Thank you for . . . for getting rid of that man. It's just—I'd rather not get the police involved, honey. Can you understand?"

Hazel frowned. "No. I mean, why not? Does my dad know that guy?" she asked. "Is he some kind of client? Is he some kind of *friend*?"

"Oh, he's no friend of your father's. I'm not even sure I would call him a client." Frankie sighed and flexed her arm gingerly. "But I have seen him before. He was here a few days ago. And he's been calling me. He says he left a painting with your dad . . . something old and valuable. He wants it back. I've been looking everywhere, but I can't find it."

"Maybe he made a mistake," suggested Hazel.

"No, no . . . I remember he did come in with a painting, and I'm pretty sure he didn't have one when he left. It wasn't very big; he carried it in a briefcase."

"What did the painting look like?" Hazel asked.

"Oh, I never saw it," Frankie replied. "I only saw the package later, after your father had wrapped it in that brown paper he always uses."

"Well, anyway, he was threatening you, Frankie.

And he talked about coming back. I think we should call the police."

"No! At least, not yet," Frankie insisted. "Something strange is going on, Hazel. I don't want to get your father into trouble. At least no more trouble than he's in already."

Hazel's throat went dry. "What makes you think my dad's in trouble?" she croaked.

"Frankie? Hazel? Where are you guys?" Ned's voice rang out from the front of the gallery.

"I have *got* to get that bell fixed," Frankie murmured.

"Back here," Hazel yelled. She turned to Frankie and whispered, "Don't say anything in front of Ned."

Frankie looked surprised but nodded.

"What a cool car," Ned said as he navigated his way among the canvases. "The guy driving it was a total jerk, though. He tried to bribe Officer Cohen, and then he tried to pretend it was all a mistake. Then, while she's writing him up for blocking the fire hydrant, this big ugly guy comes up and squeezes himself into the passenger seat. He must have been twice the size of Officer Cohen, but you could tell she made him nervous. I guess some people are just scared of cops."

"I guess," Hazel agreed. "So are they gone— Ferrari Guy and . . . Big Ugly Guy?"

Frankie gave a weak smile. "He isn't very attractive, is he?" she said. "His name is Richard C. Plevit. And he's very insistent about that middle initial."

"Well, they're gone anyway," Ned told them. "It was like they really didn't want to get another ticket. Ferrari Guy was so careful: signaling lane changes, driving half the speed limit. It was sort of funny, like watching a little old lady drive a sports car."

"Perhaps it's a good thing they met Officer Cohen, then." Frankie stood up. "And now, *this* little old lady is ready to take a break. Lunch?"

They locked the gallery and headed to Café Gentil. Ned didn't seem to notice how quiet Hazel and Frankie were; he was too busy chattering about the Ferrari.

Café Gentil occupied most of the main floor of the building where Frankie and the Frumps lived. The pastry chef who ran it was a gruff man. He loathed the tourists who thronged to his famous café, occasionally mocking them to their faces. But he had a long-standing friendship with Ned. Monsieur Gentil kept careful records of each day's baking, in an attempt to measure the effect of climate and weather conditions on the flakiness and flavor of his croissants. Ned had discovered this at the age of six and found it fascinating. They had been discussing temperature and humidity ever since.

As soon as they had ordered, and Ned had disappeared behind the counter to discuss the effect of a recent spike in air pollution, Hazel turned to Frankie.

"Why do you think my dad's in trouble?" she asked.

"Why didn't you want to talk in front of Ned?" Frankie countered.

"I didn't want to upset him," Hazel said. "He's a worrywart. You know."

Frankie nodded. "You're right. He's so clever, sometimes I forget he's just a little boy."

"So?"

"Oh. It's nothing I can put my finger on, honey. But your father had been acting strangely for a while before you and Ned came home."

"Because of Big Ugly Guy?" Hazel asked.

"Who? Oh. Mr. Plevit—Richard C. Plevit," Frankie said. "He left so many messages, I'll never forget his name. . . . No, your dad was acting oddly before Mr. Plevit showed up. I think it was something to do with Ned."

Hazel swallowed.

"*Ned?*" Her voice came out in a sort of squeak.

"Yes. That's why I wondered why you didn't want to talk in front of him. I wondered if your father had said anything to you."

"No. About what?"

"Well, I don't know exactly. That's the trouble. It all started when Ned's art teacher telephoned. You know, Ned's never taken an interest in art, and the teacher knew how important that subject is to your dad. Well, I guess Ned had done a project on some obscure artist from the 1800s, and it was really fine work. Ms. McFarquhar was so impressed, she called your father to tell him about it."

Hazel stared at Frankie. An art project? Was she kidding?

"It was after that, anyway, that Colin started making a lot of phone calls overseas and spending a lot of time on the Internet. I don't know what it was all about, but I took a phone message the day before you kids came home, and it was from some Officer—"

"*Bon! Vos croissants au jambon, salades, jus, café, eau!*" Monsieur Gentil had arrived with their food and drinks, Ned at his heels.

"Thank you, Monsieur Gentil," Hazel said, taking the glass of water and passing the coffee to Frankie.

"*Oui, merci, mon ami,*" Frankie said with a flawless accent.

Monsieur Gentil gave a pleased little bow and departed.

"I wish I spoke French as well as you do," Hazel said. "I guess it helps to have traveled so much."

Frankie nodded. "It's one of my better languages. I don't do as well with languages where the alphabet is different. But French is easy."

Ned raised an eyebrow. "If you say so."

As they munched their sandwiches, Hazel studied Frankie. She looked worn-out: There were shadows under her eyes and tiny lines creasing her forehead. She was obviously worried about Colin Frump, and she'd probably been up all night painting. Hazel didn't like the thought of her heading back to the gallery alone. What if Richard C. Plevit came back?

"Frankie, you could check the gallery's voice mail from home, couldn't you?" Hazel asked.

"Sure, honey. But why?"

"Well, you've got a lot of painting still to do, and the gallery's probably going to be pretty empty this afternoon, anyway. Why don't you just leave it closed for the rest of the day?"

Frankie tilted her head to one side. She looked at Ned for a moment, then turned back to Hazel. "I think that's a good idea," she agreed. "What will you two do?"

"Oh, we'll hang out in our apartment for a bit, you know . . . read, email friends from school, that sort of thing," Hazel said airily.

"Okay, but you'll need your key back," said Frankie, fishing around in her leather satchel.

"I can't believe you lost your key to our place," Hazel said.

"Me neither." Frankie shook her head. "Honestly, these last few days I feel like everything's been turned upside down. You know I always wear my own key around my neck so I don't lose it?"

Hazel nodded. Her father had presented Frankie with a silver chain after she'd lost her apartment key for the tenth time.

"Well, I should have put the key to your apartment on the same chain," Frankie said ruefully. "But I always kept it in a safe place, and I never lost it until just the other day."

"What kind of safe place?" Hazel asked.

"Oh, a little jar beside my desk at the gallery. I even stuck a label on it—'Colin's Spare Key'—so I wouldn't forget, or get it mixed up with the key I keep for Claire Holland so I can feed her cat when she's away. But the other day when I went to check, it was gone. I can't imagine what I did with it."

"I'm sure it'll turn up," Ned said. He patted Frankie on the shoulder before heading to the bathroom. Frankie watched him go, then turned to Hazel with a wan smile.

"I'm sure he's right. But between losing the key and losing track of that painting . . . I swear, when I walked into the gallery this morning, I felt like nothing was where I left it. Nothing seemed to be in the right place. . . . Here comes Ned. Shall we say *au revoir* to Monsieur Gentil?"

Hazel and Ned sent Frankie on ahead, while they stayed behind to collect salad, quiche, and pastries from Monsieur Gentil for dinner that night. While the food was being wrapped, Monsieur Gentil told Ned about a major storm that was headed their way, and the pair was soon embroiled in a discussion about the possible effect on tomorrow's baguettes. It took Hazel some time to pry Ned loose.

By the time they entered her apartment, they expected to see Frankie happily slapping oils on the canvas tacked to her wall. Instead, the children found her sitting pensively in the armchair by the window, her knees drawn up to her chest.

Hazel felt her heart sink.

"Frankie? Is everything okay?" she asked.

Frankie sighed and unfolded herself from her chair.

"Well, there's this artist from the neighborhood who's down in New York City, having his first big show, thanks to your father. But he left one of his best works behind. It's actually back at our gallery—I saw it today. He desperately wants it for the show. I offered to have it shipped immediately, but he's insisting someone take it to him in person. He's practically in hysterics. I know your father thinks very highly of him and wants this show to go well. I can't think what to do."

"Well, why don't we take it to him?" asked Ned. "This is Canada's biggest city—New York flights leave the airport every half hour and it's a short trip. We could be back before bedtime."

"Hey, I never thought of that," Frankie said, her face brightening. "Maybe we could even stay overnight. I can charge the trip to the gallery's account. I'm sure your father wouldn't mind, under the circumstances. I could take you guys to the zoo or the Museum of Modern Art!"

"Or maybe the American Museum of Natural History," offered Ned. "I guess for Hazel we could fit in a trip to the NBA Store, or visit that basketball court she's always wanted to see—Rucker Park?"

"What do you say, Hazel?" asked Frankie. "Shall we all go?"

Hazel's heart leaped. New York would be a fantastic adventure and a great start to their summer vacation. Plus they'd be far away from Richard C. Plevit and whatever trouble her father—or Ned—had stumbled into. Hazel was about to tell Frankie it was the best idea she'd heard in a long time, when she suddenly remembered something her father had said when they'd returned home from school: Their passports had expired.

Hazel felt a keen jab of disappointment. It was like waking up and thinking it was Saturday, only to realize a split second later that it was Monday. *And* you had a dentist appointment. *And* a history test you hadn't studied for.

"It would be great—if we only had passports," Hazel said slowly. "Remember, Ned? Dad said getting them renewed was one of the things we had to do over the summer."

The light in Frankie's eyes dimmed, and Ned made a sound like a balloon slowly deflating. Hazel gave herself a moment to mourn the lost opportunity to play pickup ball in a New York playground, then shook the image from her head.

"Look, we'll all get to New York someday, I'm sure. But in the meantime, Frankie, why don't you go? You've got a passport, right? And Ned's right, flights do leave every half hour for New York City. It's two P.M. now. You can be there by dinner and back here by . . . well, maybe not bedtime, but before the airport closes, anyway. We'll be fine on our own until you get back. "

"Yeah, don't worry about us," Ned said, holding the quiche aloft. "We've even got dinner organized."

"But what if I can't get back tonight?" Frankie asked. "The airports have been crazy lately with all the security alerts. And the weather forecast isn't great, either. What if my flight home is delayed? What if they close the airport?"

"What if this artist guy sues Dad for wrecking his big show and killing his career?" Ned replied.

"Oh, I'm sure he wouldn't do something like that," Frankie said. But her voice was uncertain.

"Can we risk it?" Hazel gave Frankie a meaningful look. "Dad seems to have a lot going on right now. We wouldn't want anyone making trouble for him."

"There *will* be some very important people from the art world at this opening," Frankie said slowly.

After a few more minutes of wavering, Frankie gave in, although she made Hazel and Ned promise to call Claire Holland or Monsieur Gentil if they needed anything. Ned used Frankie's computer to book her on a 4:30 P.M. flight to New York, while Hazel helped her locate her passport in the messy little room she called her home office. They both watched and waved from her living room window as the taxi pulled away.

"She *will* remember to stop by the gallery and actually pick up the painting, won't she?" Ned asked.

"Oh, sure. But will she pick up the *right* painting?"

They looked at each other and grinned.

"I know we said we'd sleep here, but we don't need to hang out here the whole time, especially with Frankie gone," Ned said. "Why don't we go back to our place? I've got something I'd kind of like to finish before . . . well, before . . ."

"Before my birthday?" Hazel asked.

"I cannot answer that," Ned replied, raising one eyebrow, "on grounds I might incriminate myself."

Hazel couldn't help laughing at his expression, even as she wondered what Ned had in store for her. But hanging out in their apartment was just what she wanted. With any luck, Ned would be so engrossed in his birthday project, she wouldn't see or hear from him for hours. Hours she could spend safely snooping. "Okay, let's go," she said.

Once inside their apartment, Ned headed straight for his room. "Let me know when you want to eat dinner," he said over his shoulder.

Perfect, Hazel told herself. Alone at last.

She made a quick stop in her own room, but there were no emails from her father on her computer, just a fax from Alysha, one of Hazel's oldest friends. Alysha had lived in the building with her parents until just last year, when her mother had accepted a position as head of the art department at a school in Paris. Alysha liked to fax Hazel funny pictures and articles torn from French magazines and newspapers. But Hazel had no time to waste looking at a cartoon now.

As she walked down the hall toward Colin Frump's study, Hazel became aware of a curious feeling on the back of her neck. As she turned the knob and pushed open the study door, she shivered slightly.

Don't be such a baby, Hazel thought. She squared her shoulders and stepped inside. But what she saw froze her in her tracks.

Colin Frump's study, which had been so messy and overflowing with art and books and papers just yesterday, was now as neat and empty as a classroom in August. The piles of paintings were gone. The statues she'd nearly tripped over had vanished.

Hazel's legs began to tremble so fiercely, she wasn't sure she could walk. Somehow she made it to the screen that divided her father's work space from his sitting area. His desk and chair were still there, and that was a good thing, because Hazel found she suddenly needed to sit down. Everything else was gone: the computer monitors, hard drives, the printers, the files, and the masses and masses of papers.

It was as if they had never been there.

Hazel wasn't sure how long she sat, dumbfounded, staring at the empty room. The only things left on her father's desk were a couple of empty trays labeled *Correspondence* and a small jar filled with paper clips.

Hazel's gaze focused on the jar. It reminded her of something. Something Frankie had said.

Her eyes widened: the key. Someone must have taken the key to their apartment from the jar on Frankie's desk in the gallery. Someone had used that key to break in here and steal . . . everything.

But why take *everything?* The art she could understand; it was valuable. But why take the papers and the computers?

Hazel wished that she'd read those emails when she'd had the chance. She wondered whether someone else was reading them right now.

Hazel stood up. What if that someone came back? What if it was Richard C. Plevit, or Ferrari Guy? In fact, it was probably more than one person—there would have been so much stuff to carry, heavy stuff. What if it was more than two people?

If they had a key, they could come back anytime. They could be coming up the stairs, riding the elevator right now. What if they were still in the apartment? Hazel hadn't checked any of the other rooms . . . she'd just come straight here. She flew down the hallway to Ned's room. As she neared his door, she could hear him tapping away at his keyboard. It was the greatest sound she'd ever heard. There was no time to waste in knocking; she burst through the door, calling his name.

"Hazel?" Ned tried to block her view of the monitor with his body. "What are you doing? You'll wreck the surprise!"

"We have to get out of here *now*!" Hazel grabbed his hand and pulled him out of their apartment and across the hall to safety.

4

Hazel was in the tower room again. She could feel the stone floor beneath her cheek. She could see the stars through the high, arched window. Her legs were numb and lifeless. She tried to move but couldn't. She was trapped, helpless.

Enough—enough of this stupid dream, Hazel told herself. I'm waking up—now!

"Wait. Stay."

Whoa. This was new: a voice. Nobody else had ever appeared in this dream before. Hazel was always alone.

"Who are you?" demanded Hazel.

Silence. Hazel twisted her neck, trying to see more of the tower. As far as she could tell, she was still alone. However, the room wasn't quite as empty as she'd always thought. She could see sheets or cloths draped over . . . over what? Furniture? She couldn't tell. Yet the shapes were oddly familiar.

"Can you at least tell me why I'm here?" Hazel asked. "Why do I have to wait? Why do I need to stay?"

She didn't really expect an answer. So when the woman's voice came again, shock ran through Hazel's body.

"This is where you need to be."

The voice was firm, but gentle—not angry—so Hazel decided to try again.

"Okay . . . but why? Why here? Where am I? What is this place?"

There was a long pause. Now the voice was so quiet, it was almost a whisper. It sounded like the wind sighing in the trees. It sounded sad.

"Home."

A clap of thunder jolted Hazel awake. She wasn't in the tower—she was curled up in Frankie's armchair by the window. Rain was streaming down the glass outside, and the sky was as dark as night, but Hazel's sports watch showed it was Friday, 7:00 A.M.

Hazel yawned and stretched. She was tired, and her legs ached from being folded up in the chair. It had been a long night. Her first thought had been to call

51

the police, but then she'd remembered that Frankie hadn't wanted them involved. If Colin Frump was in trouble, Hazel didn't want to make things worse for him. She'd decided to let Frankie figure out what to do.

She'd also decided it would be better not to worry Ned unnecessarily. She didn't tell him about her previous snooping or the emails she'd found or the way Richard C. Plevit had threatened Frankie at the gallery. She told her brother only about the burglary, claiming she'd entered Colin Frump's study because the door was open, and found it ransacked. Then she had paced the floor of Frankie's apartment, anxious for her return.

And then, because this was the way everything seemed to be working lately, Frankie had not returned.

It wasn't Frankie's fault, of course. In fact, when she phoned to say her fears of a storm had come true and she was stuck in New York, Frankie was so worried and guilt stricken about having left them alone that it was difficult to get a word in edgewise. Finally Ned had put his hand over the receiver and whispered to Hazel, "We can't tell—she'll have a heart attack!" and Hazel had simply nodded. There was no point in making Frankie hysterical—not when she was so far away.

But after they'd hung up, Hazel had looked at Ned

and felt the mantle of responsibility settle heavily around her shoulders. What had she gotten herself into? She'd succeeded, only too well, in keeping Ned from worrying; soon she was watching him snore contentedly, while she checked and rechecked the locks on Frankie's door. Hazel couldn't help feeling peeved. Perhaps she should wake her brother up and tell him about Plevit, or ask him about the emails. She'd see how easy he found sleep then. But no, that would be wrong.

Every muscle in Hazel's body tensed whenever she heard a noise; she'd never realized how much noise the old pipes in the building made, or how eerie the wind could sound as it whistled through the streets below.

On the phone, Hazel had been impressed by her own ability to sound calm and confident as she reassured Frankie. That pride in her bravery and maturity had lingered for a while, even after Ned's infuriating snores filled the room. But it gradually ebbed, replaced by uncertainty and, eventually, anger. Hazel realized part of her had hoped Frankie would just *know* that something was wrong, without being told. Why were grown-ups so quick to believe kids who said everything was okay? Why hadn't Frankie *guessed* Hazel was just being brave? Hazel banished that thought as unfair. None of this was Frankie's fault—she was trying so hard to help the Frumps, to keep the gallery and Colin's reputation intact. And after all, it was Hazel and Ned who had insisted she go to New York in the first place.

No, it wasn't *Frankie* who had truly put them in this situation. It wasn't Frankie who had abandoned them. But Hazel refused to take that thought any further.

Now a bolt of lightning split the angry sky, lighting up the street below. Her ears ringing from the thunder that followed, Hazel peered down at a lone car splashing through a puddle that stretched from one curb to another, sending up great spurts of water. If there had been any pedestrians around, they would have been drenched. But the sidewalks were deserted. Hazel and Ned were marooned. Alone.

"Looks like a good morning to stay indoors."

Ned had joined Hazel by the window.

"I mean, so long as the bad guys don't come back," he added.

Hazel looked at him.

"You have to admit this is way more interesting than most people's summer vacations," he said.

Hazel shook her head. Interesting, yes. But what was wrong with comfortable? What was wrong with safe? Clearly it was time Hazel and Ned had a little chat. She needed to know more about that art project

Frankie had mentioned—and Ned's website. What exactly was he up to with his chemistry club? Could he already know that this Inspector O'Toole was investigating him?

This really was a ridiculous situation. It was all very well to be nearly twelve, practically a teenager, but disappearing dads and absentee babysitters and Interpol and burglars were more than she should be expected to handle.

Still, someone had to take charge.

"C'mon. Breakfast," Hazel said firmly. "We've got OJ and slightly stale croissants and . . . there's gotta be some cereal somewhere."

"It happens all the time," Ned continued, as Hazel rummaged through Frankie's kitchen. "Thieves break in, they steal stuff like televisions and CD players, and then they come back after you've replaced them, so they can steal the brand-new ones."

Hazel gaped at her brother. How had she never noticed it before? Ned wasn't a genius. He was a *criminal* genius. She took a deep breath.

"Okay, that does make sense, sort of, but Ned, they stole art out of Dad's study," Hazel said. "That's not something you can just replace, like a television or a CD player."

"You said they also took his computer," Ned pointed out. "They'd expect him to replace that.

Anyway, maybe that was all they could carry the first time. Maybe now they'll come back for the television."

Hazel shook her head in disbelief.

"This is *soooo* not the way I planned to spend summer vacation," she muttered. Hazel shoved a bowl and several half-empty boxes of cereal in front of Ned and began tearing pieces off a croissant to quiet her growling stomach. Ned tilted his head to one side and gazed at her earnestly.

"Hazel, here's the thing I'm trying to say," he began. "The bad guys obviously got into our apartment using Frankie's spare key, which they stole from the jar on her desk in the gallery, right?"

"No kidding," Hazel said through a mouthful of croissant.

"My point is, these keys give you access to the elevator as well. So I don't think we're entirely . . . how shall I put this . . . *safe* staying here at Frankie's. I mean, unless you *want* to run into the burglars in the hall when they come back."

Hazel flashed a quick look at Ned, but he didn't seem frightened or even troubled by his own words.

"We could go find a locksmith and get the keys changed," Hazel suggested. "I mean, the locks and the keys."

"I think because the elevator's involved it's more complicated than that," Ned said. "I think maybe we need to find another place to stay. . . . Maybe we should ask Claire Holland if we could hang with her for now. And when Frankie gets back, the three of us should probably check into a hotel. Using aliases."

Hazel surveyed her brother through narrowed eyes. He really seemed to be enjoying himself.

"Room service, Hazel," Ned said dreamily. "Think of the room service!"

Hazel grinned. A hotel with Frankie did sound promising. But until Frankie returned, maybe Ned was right. Maybe they should find another adult. And stick close.

"Okay. Let's call Claire and see if we can stay with her," Hazel said.

But there was no answer at the sculptor's apartment. Hazel left a message anyway, asking her to call them at Frankie's.

"What is it with the adults in this building?" Ned asked. "It's like they're disappearing, one by one."

Before Hazel could respond, the phone rang. For a second, she wondered whether it was Claire Holland, but despite bursts of static caused by the thunderstorm, the voice at the other end was unmistakably Frankie's.

"I just wanted to make sure you kids were okay after spending the night on your own," she was saying.

"We survived, Frankie," Hazel said. "Don't worry.

When are you coming home?"

"The flights are all messed up, but I'm on the first one I could get," Frankie replied. Hazel could hear the apology in her voice.

"That's okay. So, will you be back by dinner or by bedtime?" Hazel asked.

"Er . . . bedtime," Frankie admitted reluctantly. "But you can reach me here at the hotel all day. In fact, why don't you check in with me every few hours, just so I know you're all right?"

After promising to call soon, Hazel hung up. Then the pair headed downstairs to Monsieur Gentil's café. He was bustling behind the counter, struggling to keep up with the demands of the sodden tourists who filled the tables. The sight of everyone going about their lives was relaxing, Hazel decided. In fact, just the sight of Monsieur Gentil was reassuring. Hazel gave a tiny, embarrassed laugh as she realized part of her had actually wondered if Monsieur Gentil might have disappeared as well.

Ned busied himself by clearing away the dishes left by the previous customer. He borrowed the waiter's rag to clean off the table. Then he turned to Hazel and fixed her with a very serious look.

"We need to talk," Ned said. "I want to know whatever you know about where Dad is and what's going on."

Hazel's eyes widened, then narrowed. "What makes you think I know anything?" she asked.

"You and Frankie were talking about something when we were in here yesterday, and she seemed pretty upset. Plus you've been climbing the walls since before the burglary," Ned answered. "I've been pretty patient, but time's up. Spill!"

"Deal," Hazel replied. "So long as you tell me about your website and your art project and whatever you've been cooking up with that chemistry club."

Hazel sat back and crossed her arms, studying her brother's face. He didn't look startled or defensive or angry or fearful or any of the things she'd expected. He certainly didn't look guilty.

The only thing he did look was . . . confused.

"What the heck are you talking about? What website?"

"You know," said Hazel.

Ned shook his head slightly.

"Hazel, I don't *have* a website; I've never had a website. If you want me to help you start one or something, I guess I could. But you know, I think right now we've got bigger things to worry about: Dad's disappeared, we've been burgled, and we pretty much seem to be on our own."

"Okay, forget the website. What about the chemistry club?" Hazel asked.

"Well, okay. Yeah, I've been using the club to help me design your birthday present. But it's not quite finished yet. Anyway, it's Friday. Your birthday's not until next Wednesday. Don't you want to wait and see what it is then?"

Ned's voice had a patient, condescending tone. It was really starting to bug Hazel. *She* wasn't the problem here.

"Look, Ned. I didn't want to tell you this before." Hazel drew a deep, steadying breath. "But . . . you know when I went into Dad's study yesterday? It wasn't the first time. I went in there on Wednesday, while you were working in your room. I wanted to try to find out why he took off like that."

Ned said nothing, but he raised one eyebrow.

"I know, we're not supposed to go in there," she continued. "But it's a good thing I did, because now everything's gone. And the thing is, Ned, when I was in the first time, well . . . I think I found some clues!"

Ned leaned forward. He peered intently at Hazel. "What kind of clues?"

"For starters, I found some emails Dad hadn't opened yet, and one of them was from Interpol, from an Inspector O'Toole. And the heading on the message was something about his investigation into your website. So there!"

Hazel had been hoping to see the color drain from

Ned's face, but he just looked baffled—interested, but baffled.

"Hazel, honest, I don't have a website. I don't know what the Interpol guy would be talking about."

At least the patronizing tone had disappeared from his voice.

Hazel took another deep breath. "Ned, you're not . . . you're not building some sort of bomb or something with that chemistry club, are you?"

For the first time, Hazel saw a flicker of something in her brother's eyes. Was it guilt?

"Not exactly," he said. But he looked down at the table.

"What, then?" Hazel whispered.

"I'll show you as soon as we're done here," Ned told her. "It'll mean going back into our apartment, though—just for a minute. And it'll wreck the birthday surprise."

Hazel nodded. She certainly didn't want to wait for her birthday to find out what Ned had been up to. As for returning to their apartment, she wasn't looking forward to that, but at least it was daylight now.

Monsieur Gentil hadn't been surprised to see the children at eight A.M.—he knew all about Frankie's cooking. He didn't know, of course, that Ned and Hazel had already eaten, and set a plate down in front of them. They each picked up a croissant and took a

61

bite—there was something awfully comforting about chocolate-filled pastries. The café was so busy that Monsieur Gentil had no time for talk of croissants and weather. That was fine with Ned. He just wanted Hazel to keep talking. When she told him about Richard C. Plevit and the missing painting, Ned almost choked on his *pain au chocolat*.

"I can't believe you guys didn't tell me about this," he said, his voice tight with anger.

"You're right," Hazel said. "I'm sorry."

Ned opened his mouth to speak, then closed it again.

"There are just way too many secrets here," Hazel went on. "So from now on, I think we should promise to be straight with each other about everything."

Hazel had planned to talk to Monsieur Gentil before they left, to tell him about Frankie being delayed in New York. It was high time some responsible adult knew about their situation. But Monsieur Gentil was terribly busy, and clearly not in a chatty mood. Besides, she really wanted to see what her brother had been working on.

When the children reached the door to their apartment, they found it slightly ajar. Hazel hesitated, until Ned pointed out that they might have left it open themselves, in their haste to escape yesterday. He was probably right; she had no memory of stopping to close or lock the door behind them.

Now she gave the heavy door a gentle shove and listened.

"Oh, come on," Ned said, pushing past her. "Let's get this over with."

Once inside Ned's room, Hazel closed the door behind her and leaned against it. She found herself studying his window, wondering whether they could escape that way if Richard C. Plevit suddenly appeared. Ned, meanwhile, headed to his closet and pulled out a plain cardboard shoe box with the words CAUTION! DO NOT OPEN ON PAIN OF DEATH scrawled across its top.

"This is what I've been working on," he told her, yanking off the lid. "So, happy birthday."

Hazel took a step forward and peered inside the box. She looked at Ned. "What is it?"

For answer, Ned switched on his computer and, with a few keystrokes, summoned up a website.

"This is what the chemistry club's been helping me build," he told Hazel. "We call it NIDS."

" 'Ned's Incredibly Disgusting Stinkbomb,' " Hazel read aloud. " 'Guaranteed to clear a classroom in six seconds flat and leave it uninhabitable for up to twenty-four hours.' "

She stared at her brother.

"Remember how you told me about the practical jokes some of the other girls in your dormitory were playing this year, and how everyone was always trying to find ways to get out of class?" Ned asked. "I thought a stink bomb could come in handy for next year—like when you're trying to get out of a test or something. The only thing is, the stuff they sell in joke shops isn't very good. So I decided to make something myself. Well—with the club's help.

"It's really, really awful, Hazel. I mean, it's probably the best thing I've ever done. I started working on this back when I was at school, and one went off accidentally in the lab. You wouldn't believe the smell. They had to close the room for two days! Luckily, I knew enough to get out of there fast. My skin didn't have time to really absorb the smell. I did have to burn my shirt, though. . . ." Ned's voice trailed off, his eyes aglow with happiness.

Hazel didn't know what to say.

"Wow," she said finally. "Uh . . . thanks. I'm sure it's what all the cool kids will be taking to school next year."

"It's completely harmless," Ned assured her. "I mean, it's not actually poisonous or anything. Of course, it can cause vomiting, itchy eyes, skin rashes . . . but nothing *permanent*."

"Sometimes I'm really not sure we're even related,"

Hazel said, shaking her head. "Come on. Let's get out of here."

"Should I bring the bomb?" Ned asked. "I can finish it at Frankie's. You never know, it might come in handy—especially if the bad guys come back."

"Sure, whatever," said Hazel, rolling her eyes.

As they walked toward the door, Hazel recalled her dream from the night before. Maybe Ned's theory had finally been proved wrong. Instead of something bad happening, she'd found out something good: Ned wasn't building a bomb. Not a real one, anyway. A stink bomb—even an Incredibly Disgusting one— hardly qualified.

"Hey, before we go, should we check to see whether Dad's sent you an email?" Ned asked.

Hazel didn't want to linger in their apartment any longer than they had to, but a message from their father was probably worth the risk. She nodded and headed for her room.

There were half a dozen emails from friends— mostly kids from school wanting to compare summer vacations—but nothing from their father.

"I can read those later," she told Ned. "Let's go."

"Wait. What's that?" Ned asked, pointing to a paper beside Hazel's computer. "A fax from Alysha?"

Hazel was about to tell her brother they had no time for comics or cartoons, but a quick glance showed there was nothing amusing about this fax. Across the top of the clipping, Alysha had written:

> *Hazel! I found this newspaper in the street. I can't read Turkish but it doesn't look good. I hope this is all a big mistake. I tried calling, but there was no answer. I hope you get this. Call me! Love, A.*

Hazel couldn't read the clipping either, of course. But her hands were shaking as she stared at the fax. Two grainy photographs accompanied the text. The smaller picture looked remarkably like Ferrari Guy, although she couldn't be absolutely sure.

But there was no mistaking the identity of the man in the larger photograph. That man—the one with the unshaven face and wild eyes, the one in handcuffs and a prisoner's uniform—that man was definitely their father.

"**F**rankie, why would anyone put Dad in prison?" Hazel shouted into the phone. "Where is he? And why is Ferrari Guy in the story too? What does it say about him?"

Even though Frankie had lived in Istanbul for a semester when she was a student, it was taking her a long time to read the copy Hazel and Ned had just faxed to her hotel in New York. At least, it seemed to Hazel that it was taking a long time.

"I'm sorry, kids. My Turkish is a little rusty." Frankie's voice sounded rusty too, Hazel thought, like she was having a hard time getting the words out. "It seems there's some sort of art scandal involving important galleries in Turkey and Cyprus. The article talks about arrests being made in connection with smuggling and . . . I guess that word means *fraud* or *fake*. There's a long list of names in this one section— I think they're talking about artists whose work was forged or something. I've really got to go find someone who can help me translate this more precisely."

"What does it say about Dad?" Ned asked, his voice quiet. He was standing in the doorway of Frankie's kitchen, listening on the extension.

"Not much, I'm afraid. They've arrested him for something to do with this art fraud or whatever, and they're searching for the man in the other photograph. They seem to think he's your father's partner or something."

"You mean Ferrari Guy? The guy who drove off with Richard C. Plevit?" asked Hazel.

"I didn't see him yesterday," Frankie answered. "I only saw Mr. Plevit. But if this man in the picture is the one you saw *with* Mr. Plevit . . . well, then I'm really confused."

"Why?" asked Hazel. Her mouth was dry; her tongue seemed to be made of cotton balls.

"Well, the man you call Ferrari Guy is identified here as Clive Pritchard."

"So?" Ned asked.

"It's just that the paper says this Clive Pritchard is your father's partner—partner in crime, I guess— although I really need help with some of this vocabulary.

But I've never seen him before."

"Well, then that's good, right? I mean, the paper's wrong—the Turkish police have made a mistake," Hazel said.

"Yeah . . ." Frankie's voice trailed away.

"What?" Ned asked. "*What?*"

"It's probably nothing. But I recognize his name from somewhere . . . Clive Pritchard, I mean. I think your father does know him . . . or maybe Colin *used* to know him a long time ago. But I have the impression your dad really doesn't like him. There's no way they'd be partners . . . or friends. More like enemies."

For a few moments Hazel and Ned were silent, staring at each other across the room. The only noise was the faint sound of paper rustling on the other end of the phone as Frankie continued to read.

"What are we going to do?" Hazel whispered. She was speaking to Ned, but it was Frankie who answered, and for once she didn't seem flustered at all.

"Look, kids, I'm not going to come home," Frankie said. "This will be one of the weirdest expenses I've ever billed your dad for, but I'm catching the next flight to Istanbul, as soon as the storm lets up. I've still got a few friends there, and your father's going to need a lawyer. But you can't be alone. Not with Richard C. Plevit hanging around. You'd better ask Claire Holland if you can stay with her for a few days. You can ignore the cat, Ned, right?"

Hazel looked at Ned. He raised one eyebrow. If they told Frankie about the break-in, she'd probably feel she had to come home. But now it seemed Colin Frump needed her help more than they did. *Somebody* had to go rescue him.

For a moment, Hazel considered telling Frankie she and Ned had to go to Istanbul too. But they didn't have passports.

"Sure, Frankie, we'll be okay," Hazel said. Ned nodded silently. Hazel was on the verge of pointing out that Frankie couldn't hear a nod over the phone when she realized her brother was trying to reassure *her*. She managed a weak grin in response.

"Frankie, make sure you get Dad a good lawyer," Ned said. "Get the best one in Istanbul, no matter what it costs."

"Of course," Frankie said. "I promise I'll get to the bottom of this. Your father is a good man, and whatever he's mixed up in, it's not his fault. We'll fix it, okay?"

We'll fix it? Hazel loved her neighbor, but she wasn't all that sure Frankie was up to the task.

"Okay, Frankie," Hazel said. "Is there anything that Ned and I can do in the meantime? We could go to the gallery and look for clues or something. . . ."

"No! Stay away from the gallery," Frankie ordered.

"I don't want you bumping into that Plevit man or this Pritchard guy, either. If you want to help . . . well, your father has an old friend at the Royal Canadian Museum: Ludwig Barta. He's the curator of the Mediterranean department. I know Colin went to see him before he left. Maybe it wouldn't hurt for you to go talk to him. He might even have some contacts in Turkey who could help me."

"Okay, we'll go right now," said Hazel. "We can get there before lunch."

"But promise me first that you'll go see Claire and let her know what's going on. You don't have to tell her everything. Just enough so that she understands you need a place to stay, okay?"

Hazel and Ned agreed, and Frankie promised to call again as soon as she could.

But there was still no answer at Claire Holland's apartment.

The children trooped downstairs to Café Gentil. It was eleven o'clock.

"Back again? I must try once more to have Frankie take the cooking classes." Monsieur Gentil sighed. "*Rien de compliqué, n'est-ce pas?* Just some simple omelettes—you know? Fresh ingredients, plain food."

"Actually, Frankie's not here right now," Ned said. "Do you know where Claire Holland is?"

"Ah, Claire. Now she is a much better cook," said

71

Monsieur Gentil. "But she is away just now, at one of those—how do you say it—an artists' retreat, they call it, with the fresh air and butterflies. She is in the mountains. She took her cat."

Ned looked like he was about to explode. Hazel grabbed his arm and smiled at Monsieur Gentil.

"We have to go. But we'll be back for dinner. See you!"

Before Ned or the old man could speak, Hazel had bundled her brother out the door and into the street-car that had just pulled up outside.

"What's the hurry?" Ned asked indignantly. "I was only going to point out that the adults in this building can't seem to stay put, that's all. Besides, I'm hungry."

"You're always hungry," Hazel answered. "And I didn't want you blabbing about everything to Monsieur Gentil."

A flush crept across Ned's cheeks.

"I. Never. Blab. And anyway, we can trust Monsieur Gentil."

"I'm beginning to think we can't trust anybody," said Hazel.

They glared at each other and didn't talk again until they were standing in front of the museum. The rain had stopped, but it had left a chill in the air and the sky was still dark, blanketed by ominous clouds. Staring up at the museum, Hazel shivered. It was an imposing gray building, built to impress passersby in the early 1900s, and the years had done nothing to wear down its hauteur. Even the pigeons gathering on the carved stone lintels and broad steps seemed to sniff as they stared at the two of them.

"I think if we go in the side door, we can ask where the offices are," Hazel said.

But the receptionist there stared at them coldly.

"The dinosaur exhibit is at the front of the building, just off the atrium," he informed them.

"We're not here for dinosaurs," Ned said hotly.

"I see. Well, lost children are supposed to report to the coat-check desk."

"We're here to see Mr. Ludwig Barta, please," Hazel said, elbowing Ned aside before he could speak again.

"Do you have an appointment?"

Hazel made her face a polite mask. "Yes, of course," she replied.

"Really?" The receptionist looked disbelieving. "Mr. Barta is a busy man. He doesn't normally meet with . . . *children*."

Hazel stiffened.

"Actually, our father is the one with the appointment," Ned said. "He wanted to discuss some donation he's thinking of making. What was it, Hazel, a new wing or something?"

Hazel swallowed. "I think it was more like a gallery. Something to do with Mediterranean studies, anyway."

She smiled daggers at the man.

"We're supposed to meet our dad here, but I guess we're early. I hope he shows up soon. We're all having lunch at the Plaza."

"And what is your father's name?" asked the receptionist icily.

"Colin Frump," said Ned, and then jumped as a hand clapped him on the shoulder.

"Colin Frump? Brilliant! I've been trying to reach him, but he's not answering his cell phone."

Hazel whipped around to see an elderly, bearded man in a leather jacket and jeans smiling down at her. A motorcycle helmet was tucked under one arm; the other arm was already steering Ned down the hall.

"Thanks, Willie," the man called over his shoulder. "When Mr. Frump gets here, just send him on through."

"Right away, Mr. Barta."

"Dear girl, did you say something about the Plaza?" Mr. Barta asked as they turned the corner and headed down a long, dimly lit hall lined with murky oil paintings. Mr. Barta strode purposefully toward a tall, carved wooden door at the far end of the hall. Ned had to trot to keep up.

"Yep—soon as our dad gets here," Ned said smoothly. "Have you known him long, Mr. Barta?"

"Since before you were born," the elderly man replied, holding open the door with a courteous gesture. "And I've always wanted to meet you two. This way; my office is just up these stairs, down the hall, and around the corner."

Hazel marveled at the silence as Mr. Barta led them down a hallway that was padded with Persian carpets and illuminated by tiny, twinkling lights. As they rounded the corner, they entered a waiting area complete with elegant gilt chairs. Mr. Barta unlocked a door marked LUDWIG BARTA and ushered them inside.

It was one of the oddest offices Hazel had ever seen. A sarcophagus leaned against a corner of the fireplace mantel, and a giant beetle in a glass jar was being used as a paperweight atop a stack of papers that teetered on the edge of the curator's desk.

"Now," Mr. Barta began, "do we expect your father soon? I need to speak with him. Urgently."

Hazel looked at Ned. Just then, a buzzing sound filled the room.

"Excuse me, I have to take this," Mr. Barta said, turning his back to the children as he opened his cell phone.

Ned stepped closer to Hazel. "We never discussed what to say," he hissed. "What if he thinks we're nuts? What if he's not on Dad's side?"

"Don't panic," Hazel whispered. "He seems nice, and Frankie said he was Dad's old friend, remember? We'll just tell him . . . everything."

Mr. Barta turned back to face them.

"Oh, dear. Children, I have to leave you for a few moments. So sorry. Make yourselves comfortable, and if your father arrives before I get back, tell him I'll be with you presently."

In the doorway, Mr. Barta paused and gave them a warm smile. "I really am delighted to meet you both. Did you know it was your mother who introduced me to Colin? Such a lovely woman, your mother."

Hazel blinked. Mr. Barta had known their mother?

"Saved by the cell," Ned observed. "Now, before he gets back, how exactly do you plan to explain everything that's going on and find out what he knows and get him to help Dad, when *we* don't even know what's going on or what kind of help Dad needs?"

"Calm down, Ned." But Hazel's own heart was thumping. Maybe Mr. Barta could help them learn more about their mom, too. She took a deep breath.

"Look, Ned, we trust Frankie, right? Well, Frankie obviously trusts Mr. Barta, or she wouldn't have sent us here. She said Dad visited him recently, so we'll just explain that Dad's in trouble, and we need to know what they talked about and whether it had anything to do with this mess."

"Frankie trusts everyone," Ned pointed out. "And didn't you say we shouldn't even trust Monsieur Gentil?"

"You're right," Hazel admitted. "But do you have a better idea? I mean, isn't this why we came here in the first place? Besides, he just said he knew our mother."

Ned was silent for a few moments. Then he shrugged.

"I guess so. Okay . . . tell him everything. I guess we have to trust someone sooner or later."

He threw himself down into a squashy armchair and stuck his legs out straight in front of him, studying his sneakers.

"Lunch at the Plaza?" Ned queried after a few moments. He raised an eyebrow.

"I think that was more believable than a whole new wing." But Hazel thumped his shoulder affectionately before throwing herself into the armchair next to Ned's. "Still, pretty quick thinking, Squirt."

"Yes it was," Ned agreed smugly. He added as an afterthought, "Of course, Dad probably *could* afford to pay for a whole new wing."

"Oh, I don't think he's all *that* rich," Hazel said, gazing at a stuffed eagle perched on the corner of a bookcase at the far end of the room. It appeared to have a stuffed mouse hanging out of its beak.

"Trust me, he is," Ned replied.

Something about his voice dragged Hazel's attention away from the bird. "What do you know that I don't know?" she asked.

"Hey, can I help it if I stumble across a few computerized bank statements when I'm minding my own business, working on my decrypting program?" he queried.

"You're kind of scary, you know that?" Hazel asked.

Ned grinned. "I'm going to the bathroom. I saw a door marked MEN just outside in the waiting room."

"You can run but you can't hide!" Hazel called as the door closed behind her brother.

Alone in the strange room, Hazel's thoughts were anything but quiet. If Ned had been snooping in their father's financial affairs, maybe he'd also looked into their family history. If he knew anything about their mom, would he have told her?

The sound of voices raised in argument was coming from down the hall. Hazel opened the door a crack. She couldn't see anyone yet, but the voices were getting nearer.

"I don't care if he's with somebody. I want to see him!"

Hazel knew that low, threatening voice.

"Please, sir, I'm afraid if you don't come with me, I will have to call security. Mr. Barta is expecting a very important donor any minute. He can't be disturbed."

The second voice sounded like the receptionist. But that first voice was definitely Richard C. Plevit. They were coming down the hall. As soon as they turned the corner, they'd see her.

Hazel bolted for the men's room. Ned was washing his hands at the sink. Apart from the two of them, the room was deserted.

"Hazel, what are you doing in here? This is a *men's* room!" Ned hissed. "Get out before you get us into real trouble!"

"We're already in *real* trouble, Ned," Hazel said. "Richard C. Plevit is coming down the hall."

Ned joined Hazel at the door. The receptionist was arguing with Plevit.

"Well, I'm not going anywhere; I'll wait until his meeting's done," Richard C. Plevit said. They heard the antique chair creak as he sat down.

Hazel looked at Ned in horror. Richard C. Plevit was blocking their only way out.

"How long before the receptionist tells him a couple of kids are with Mr. Barta?" she whispered.

"How long before they realize no one's in there?" Ned asked.

"That would actually be okay. Then they'd leave," said Hazel. But that hope was dashed the next moment.

"Hey, buddy, where's the men's room?" Richard C. Plevit asked.

Ned grabbed Hazel's arm. She glanced around the small, bare room. Where could they hide? There were two sinks, two urinals, and two stalls. She and Ned could hide in one of the stalls. But then again, maybe that wasn't such a good idea: Hazel didn't really want to be trapped in a men's room with Richard C. Plevit. What if he found them?

The air was suddenly filled with a loud clanging. Hazel looked at Ned. He had broken the glass fire alarm cover and pulled the lever. Without saying a word, her brother crossed the room and cranked open the window. Climbing up on the radiator, he was able to get his head and shoulders outside. He turned and beckoned to Hazel.

"Come on," he said.

They were on the second floor. Did Ned expect her to jump? Did he *want* her to break her leg? Her neck? They'd be better off taking their chances with Richard C. Plevit! Surely the man would leave now that the alarm had been sounded. Couldn't they just head for a fire escape and disappear into the crowd?

The window overlooked Wodehouse Way, a

meandering arboretum that led from the back of the museum to the university campus nearby. And Ned was gesturing toward a stately, spreading maple tree positioned just outside the window.

If it hadn't been an emergency, Hazel would have refused. Although the tree's limbs were broad and inviting, they weren't quite close enough to reach. Besides, they were still slick from the rain. You had to jump—and grab—and she knew there was a distinct possibility that one of them might miss and tumble to the grass below.

Ned had already hoisted himself onto the windowsill. As he crouched, poised to jump, he flashed Hazel an encouraging smile. Then he turned his head.

"Wait!"

He was gone.

Hazel rushed to the window. She half expected to see her brother lying on the ground, motionless. But he was dangling from the nearest branch, a wide grin across his face. As Hazel watched, Ned began swinging his way toward the trunk of the tree, hand over hand, as if playing on monkey bars.

"C'mon, Hazel," he called. "It's easy."

Taking a deep breath and resisting the temptation to close her eyes, Hazel climbed onto the windowsill and leaned as far out as she could before pushing off, arms outstretched. There was one terrifying moment when her feet left the sill and she could feel herself falling. But then her fingers closed around cold, wet bark. *Got it!*

Following Ned's example, Hazel began working her way toward the center of the tree, moving hand over hand. Being taller helped—her sneakers soon found a branch that could bear some of her weight. From there it was a question of keeping her eyes focused on the tree trunk and not panicking.

As they slowly lowered themselves from dripping branch to dripping branch, she kept glancing back. It wasn't just because she hated to look down. She also wanted to make sure no one was watching. But no face appeared at the window.

The alarm was still clanging, and from her vantage point, Hazel could now see museumgoers starting to file out along the boulevard to the north of the park. She gave a quick glance at her brother on the branch below her.

"Hurry up, Ned—there could be a lot of people in this park soon."

Ned nodded.

When they had both reached the lowest branch, Hazel looked down. There was still a drop of almost ten feet to the grass below.

"I'll go first this time," she told Ned. "Then I can try to catch you."

"You can go first, but I don't need anyone to *catch* me."

Hazel knelt on the sturdy branch for a few seconds, then, grasping the tree limb with both hands, she carefully lowered her body until her arms were fully extended and her feet hovered only a few feet above the grass. She hung there for a moment before letting go, remembering to bend her knees when she landed to cushion the impact.

"Look out beloooooooow!"

Hazel looked up just in time to see Ned launch himself off the bottom tree limb, sail through the air, and land in some juniper bushes. He got awkwardly to his feet, rubbing his leg.

"You know, I think this summer's turning out to be the greatest one ever!" said Ned, his eyes shining. "I've always wondered if you could get to one of those trees from the museum windows!"

"All I can say is, I'm glad Mr. Barta's office wasn't on the *third* floor." Hazel brushed grass off her T-shirt. "Or the sixth."

An older man occupying the bench beneath a nearby elm had stopped feeding the pigeons from his paper bag and was gazing at the children with interest. Hazel waved to him as if dropping out of a tree was the most normal thing in the world; then she took Ned by the arm and walked him south, toward the university. The sky was clearing, and for now they were free of Richard C. Plevit.

"You did a great job on our escape," she told Ned.

"Yeah, but the mission was pretty much a bust," he pointed out. "We didn't get to ask Mr. Barta anything, and we almost got caught by that Plevit guy. It's like he's everywhere. Who knows where he'll turn up next?"

Hazel nodded.

"Maybe we should leave town or something," Ned said. "But where would we go? It's not like we have any relatives or family that we could stay with."

Hazel felt her jaw actually drop. Ned was a genius. She, on the other hand, was a moron. How could she have forgotten about that other email on her father's computer? What was the matter with her?

"Family! That's where we'll go."

"But we don't have any other family."

"Yes we do: Oliver Frump," Hazel told him. "He wanted a family reunion; he's going to get one. All we have to do is find him."

*N*ed, of course, had never heard of Oliver Frump. Hazel explained quickly about the other unread email she'd discovered on Colin Frump's computer. Ned was stunned.

"All our lives, Dad's told us we're *it*. There's just the three of us, no one else. No other family whatsoever. And you find out we've got some relative named Oliver, and you don't even mention it? Are you nuts?"

The truth was, Hazel had been preoccupied with the possibility that Ned might be building a bomb. She could see now that her brother wasn't some evil genius, and the fact that she'd considered it, even briefly, wasn't exactly something she wanted to admit.

"There's been a lot going on. Excuse me for being focused on Interpol and the burglary and the bad guys."

It was almost one thirty, and Hazel's stomach was rumbling. She tried to distract Ned with a picnic on the west lawn of the university campus, buying hot dogs and lemonade from a street vendor. Food usually worked wonders on Ned. Usually. But not this time.

"So much for being straight with each other; so much for too many secrets," Ned said, still sulking. "You're *sure* there's nothing else you should tell me? Like, maybe we won the lottery but you just forgot to mention it?"

"I swear there's nothing else," Hazel promised. "There were two messages—the one from Inspector O'Toole about your website and another one from this Oliver Frump guy, wanting to talk to Dad about a Frump family reunion."

"I still don't get that website thing," Ned said, swallowing the last of his hot dog. "Maybe that inspector has me mixed up with some other Ned Frump. Or maybe someone's stolen my identity and they're using my good name for evil. Identity theft is a big problem these days, you know. Happens all the time."

Hazel relaxed. Ned might not have forgiven her for the oversight about Oliver Frump, but at least he was moving off the topic. They sipped their lemonade and gazed at the summer students going in and out of the elegant stone buildings.

"I wonder how this Oliver Frump guy tracked Dad down," he mused. "Do you think maybe he's a genealogist or something?"

"I dunno. Anyway, I don't have Oliver Frump's email address, so I'm not sure how we're going to find him," Hazel admitted.

"If we do find him, I hope he's a chatty guy." Ned frowned. "There's a lot of stuff I'd like to know. For instance, what happened to the rest of the family? And where does all Dad's money come from? You know, a year ago, after I, uh . . . stumbled . . . onto some data about Dad and his money, I asked him how come he was so rich."

"Seriously?" Hazel was impressed.

"He wouldn't tell me, though. *And* he made me promise not to snoop around in his affairs anymore." Ned gave Hazel a sidelong glance. "He was really serious about it. I had to *swear*."

"So I guess you never found out anything about Mom, did you? I mean anything more than what Dad's told us?"

Hazel held her breath. But Ned shook his head.

"No, I kept my promise. No more snooping."

"Hey, Ned—Dad never made *me* promise anything like that. Why wasn't he worried about *my* detecting skills?"

Ned slurped air from the bottom of his paper cup.

"He wouldn't have thought he needed to ask." Ned's tone was matter-of-fact. "You're kind of protective when it comes to Dad."

"Well, those days are over," Hazel said.

"Yeah, I don't exactly feel bound by my promise anymore, either." Ned grinned. "When your father's in jail and the bad guys are chasing you, all bets are off."

"Right."

They sat in silence for a few minutes. The air was warm and unpleasantly humid. Smog alerts had become commonplace in the past couple of years, and the pollution made Hazel's head ache.

"I really do think we should get out of town," she said. "Maybe this Oliver Frump will have some answers. I mean, maybe he knows Dad. Maybe he even knew Mom, too. I wish we knew what she was really like."

"What if we find this guy and he doesn't want us to come?" Ned asked. Now that the adrenaline of their escape had subsided, Hazel thought his voice sounded tired, even a little worried. "Or what if Oliver does invite us, but he lives in another country? We don't have passports."

Hazel felt a tug at the corner of her mind and tried to picture the email. There had been something, a French name . . . something about an island? But the more she reached for it, the more the memory wriggled away.

Hazel stood up, wadded her hot dog wrapper into a ball, and lobbed it into a nearby trash can.

"Let's just find him first," she said to her brother. "That's going to be the hard part."

But there she was completely wrong. Finding Oliver Frump proved surprisingly simple.

Hazel and Ned weren't altogether comfortable about returning to the apartment building, but they agreed that computers and telephones were needed to search for Oliver Frump. As Hazel turned the key in Frankie's door, she could hear the telephone ringing. She grabbed it before the answering machine could switch on.

"Hello?" she said breathlessly into the phone.

"Oh, Hazel, you're there!" Frankie sounded harried. "My plane leaves at two forty P.M., so I just have a few moments before I have to board. I was trying you at Claire's, but there was no answer."

"Yeah. Um, Frankie, the thing is, I think Claire's out of town," Hazel said. "I don't think we're going to be able to stay with her."

"Oh. Ohhhhhh, that's right. She was going to the mountains on that silly retreat. Maybe you could ask Monsieur Gentil—"

"No. Listen, Frankie. Ned and I think it might be a good idea for us to get out of town for a bit, or at least out of this building. We were trying to think of someone else we could stay with. . . . Do you know . . . did my dad ever mention any relatives to you? Like, maybe, somebody named Oliver Frump?"

Ned picked up the kitchen extension. There was a long silence on Frankie's end of the line. Finally she said, "Your father swore me to secrecy. I mean, I really had to swear. . . . "

"Had to swear *what*?" Hazel asked, trying to keep the impatience from her voice.

"Oh, Colin will kill me. I mean, I was only supposed to call his brother in case of emergency."

"Frankie—did you say *brother*?" Ned's voice rose.

"Do you have an actual number for Oliver?" Hazel asked.

"Oliver?" Frankie sounded confused. "I'm not sure that was his name . . . but, yes, Colin has a brother. And I'm definitely supposed to contact him only in an extreme emergency. . . ."

"Frankie! If this isn't an emergency, I don't know what is," Ned yelled. "We can't stay here anymore—our apartment's been burgled, and that Richard Plevit guy's following us all over the city!"

"What?" Frankie asked. "Oh, kids, they're calling my plane. I can't believe this! What do you mean

90

burgled? When? No—wait! What did you say about Plevit?"

"Frankie, we're okay. Get on that plane and go help Dad," Hazel said. "Just first, please, tell us how to find his brother."

"All I know is that he lives on an island, where the Saint Lawrence River meets Lake Ontario. Someplace called Land's End. His phone number is in my book, under *E*."

"*E* for *Frump*?" asked Ned. "What kind of alphabetizing system do you use?"

"*E* for *emergency*," Frankie explained.

Ned was silent.

"I could hardly file him under *F* for *Frump*," she said defensively. "Not when your father made such a big deal out of it being a secret."

"Okay, Frankie, I've found it," Hazel said. She had Frankie's address book. Under the *E* entries was written: *Emergency Contact for Colin*. There was a phone number and the words *Île du Loup*, but no street address.

"Île du Loup," Hazel muttered to herself. That was it—that was what Oliver Frump had written: family reunion on Île du Loup.

"I've got to go, darlings," Frankie was saying. "Promise you'll have Monsieur Gentil help you with all this—I don't know how long it will take you to reach your uncle, but in the meantime, Monsieur Gentil will make sure you're okay."

"Sure," Hazel agreed.

"Oh, and honey, it's Friday, and I really don't know if I can get all this sorted out and have your father home by Wednesday, so you might as well take your birthday present to your uncle's place."

"Thanks, Frankie, but you can give it to me when you get back," Hazel offered.

"Actually, *I* haven't gotten you anything yet," Frankie said, sounding faintly embarrassed. "What I meant was that you should take your birthday present from Colin. He set it aside ages ago, for when you turned twelve. It's something you've wanted for a long time."

"But Frankie, we really were burgled," Hazel said sadly. "I know you won't believe this, but everything's gone from Dad's study, really. Everything."

"What? Oh. They're telling me I have to get on the plane now," Frankie said. "No, sweetie, the painting is in my office—my *home* office. Colin gave it to me for safekeeping a few days ago. We were going to do this whole surprise party. . . . Anyway, it's in my closet, wrapped in that brown paper we use at the gallery. Take it with you. Good-bye."

After Frankie had hung up, Hazel and Ned argued briefly over which of them should be the one to make the call to Oliver Frump. A coin toss awarded the honor to Ned. He cleared his throat several times while listening to the phone ring on the other end.

"I don't think anyone's home," he whispered to Hazel, just as a recorded message began to play.

"You have reached the Frump family residence," a deep voice announced. "We can't get to the phone right now. Please leave your message and a number where you may be reached."

Ned cleared his throat again. "Hello. My name is Ned Frump and, uh, I'm looking for my uncle, Oliver Frump? A situation has arisen for my sister and me and . . . we urgently need to speak to you. In fact, we'd like to see you. To . . . visit your . . . to visit you. If that would be convenient. As soon as possible. Like, maybe today? Because, see, we need to leave town. I mean, we don't *need* to, but it would be . . . advisable. Under the circumstances."

Hazel made a face. She should have insisted on being the one to call. At least Ned remembered to leave Frankie's phone number before hanging up.

"How was I?" Ned asked. "Did I sound strange? I was really nervous. Do you think he'll call back?"

"You were fine," Hazel lied. "I'm sure when he gets that message, he'll be curious to meet you."

She headed for the closet in Frankie's home office.

"I'm going to call back and leave my email address too," Ned called after her. "In case he doesn't get my message until late tonight or something. If he thinks it's too late to call, he could always email us."

"Why not leave another message saying he can call anytime?" Hazel suggested as she rummaged through the boxes and bags piled haphazardly in Frankie's closet. "If you want to leave the email address, I guess it can't hurt."

The package, when she found it, was tucked under a sheaf of old watercolors that Frankie had stored on a high shelf. It was definitely her present. A yellow note stuck to the brown wrapping bore Colin Frump's handwriting: *For Hazel's 12th*.

Hazel lifted it down carefully and carried it out to the living room, where Ned was just replacing the telephone receiver.

"I left all our email addresses," he told her. "Yours, mine, and Frankie's, just in case. I told him we'd probably be out this afternoon, but we'd check for messages at dinnertime. Want to go get a snack at Café Gentil?"

"Sure," Hazel agreed absently. She was staring at the package.

"Are you going to open that now?" Ned asked. "You might as well. Frankie already said it was a painting, so there's not much of a surprise left."

"Yeah," replied Hazel. "And she said it was something I'd always wanted. Which is weird, because I can't think of a painting I've always wanted. I mean, I'm not really into art. Not like Dad."

Ned nodded. "That is sort of strange."

Hazel ran her fingers down the sides of the package. An odd feeling of excitement was building inside her.

"There is one thing I used to ask Dad for," Hazel said. "A picture of Mom—you know, just a photograph. Supposedly they all burned up in a house fire. But Ned, what if there was a *painting* of Mom?"

"A house fire? He told *me* some cleaners he'd hired after a party threw them out by accident."

Hazel froze. "What are you talking about? There was a fire. He must have told us a thousand times."

Ned grimaced. "Look—I don't know what he told you, but he never said anything to me about a fire."

"But" —Hazel shook her head, trying to clear it— "he did. He must have. Anyway, why would cleaners throw out photographs? You must have misunderstood."

"Or you misunderstood. If there'd been a fire, other stuff would be missing."

"Well, I don't know—maybe there *was* a fire, and he had cleaners come in afterward and the photos got thrown out because they were damaged by water or smoke or something." Hazel felt like the ground was shifting under her feet. "The important thing is—"

"Still, you wouldn't throw out all your photos after a fire, would you?" Ned continued. "It's not like they could be replaced. You'd keep them, just for sentimental purposes, because they were the only record of your children as babies, or your wife before she died. . . ."

"Well, maybe he threw them out because he still had this painting of Mom," Hazel said, "and now he's giving it to me!"

With a flourish, she ripped open the package and stared down at the small oil painting.

It was not a painting of their mother, or of anyone's mother for that matter. It was a dark landscape depicting a castle on the shores of a storm-tossed sea. The painting looked quite old; its surface was covered in hairline cracks, and something about it reminded Hazel of an exhibit her father had taken them to see.

As Hazel stared at the canvas, tears pricked at her eyes. She blinked them away, furious at herself. It was silly to feel disappointed. Colin Frump loved art so much, he probably thought she'd be thrilled to receive such a valuable painting. But why on earth had Frankie thought this was something she'd always wanted? She looked over at Ned to gauge his reaction. He was polishing his glasses.

"Well, it's certainly not what I expected," Hazel admitted.

Ned cleared his throat. "It's not what I expected, either," he replied. "Hazel, this is so weird. I care even less about art than you do, but I recognize this painting! I did a whole project on the artist who painted it!"

Hazel swallowed. Ned's art project. Frankie had said something about her father acting strangely after Ned's art teacher had contacted him about a project Ned had done for school. It hadn't made any sense at the time. It still didn't. Except—

"Ned, this painting. It's not very big. It would fit into a briefcase, wouldn't it? What if this is the one Richard C. Plevit wanted back from Frankie, from the gallery?"

"But why would Dad give it to you?" Ned asked. "For safekeeping?"

"I don't know. I don't think Dad would want to put me—well, either of us—in danger," Hazel said. "And even if he did want me to look after a painting for him, don't you think he'd just say so? I mean, he wouldn't try to pass off a stolen painting as a gift."

Hazel stared at the canvas and then at Ned, who was pacing back and forth, rubbing his glasses with the hem of his T-shirt.

"Okay, let's think about this. What do you remember about this painting? If it's the one from your project,

I mean. Who painted it? Is it valuable?"

Ned perched on the edge of the old valise that served as Frankie's coffee table.

"The painter's name was Paolo Cafazzo," Ned said. "He was some Romantic painter—as in Romanticism, with a capital *R*. He basically became my whole project."

"Why did you pick him?" Hazel asked. "Did Dad suggest him?"

"No, I never talked to Dad about it," Ned said, frowning. "We were supposed to choose someone from the Romantic period. Most of the guys picked French painters, like Eugène Delacroix, or this Géricault guy. I wanted to do someone nobody else was doing, so I spent some time on the Internet and found these websites all about him."

"Websites?" Hazel asked. Her heart was pounding.

"Sure," Ned said. "He's got some big-time fans, this Cafazzo guy. There are a couple of sites I found devoted just to him, and how he was like the greatest painter you've never heard of. And there were links to other sites, art history professors' sites, papers people had written about him."

"Show me," Hazel said. She could hardly breathe.

Ned shrugged and headed for Frankie's computer. Hazel stood behind him and watched as he entered his first website address. He made a *tsk* sound as the computer rejected his efforts, and tried again.

The room was silent but for the sound of Ned's furious typing. Again and again, he entered website names, only to be told the site could not be found. He swiveled the chair around to face Hazel.

"This is nuts!" Ned exploded. "I mean, I may not be remembering every site address exactly right, but some of those names I definitely know by heart. I know I'm entering them correctly. I don't understand how they could all just disappear!"

"What about books?" Hazel asked. "What books did you use?"

Ned looked a little embarrassed. "Well, actually," he began, "I kind of did *all* my research over the net."

"All of it?" Hazel repeated.

"Everything to do with Paolo Cafazzo, anyway," Ned said. "I mean, I used books to find out general stuff about the Romantic period, but I couldn't find anything about him in the books. It's like nobody knew about him until just recently. That's why I picked him—and I think that's why my art teacher liked the project so much. She said she'd never heard of him either, but when she checked out the sites I told her about, she was totally impressed."

Hazel looked at her brother. She felt as if she had been stuck, staring at a jigsaw puzzle for days, and all of a sudden she could see where the next pieces should go. There was so much more to figure out—so many giant gaps and so many little pieces that didn't seem to fit—but for the first time, Hazel believed they could solve it. They *would* solve it.

"Ned. I think I know what the inspector meant in his message to Dad," she said. "When he said 'Ned's website,' he didn't mean a site you *made*. He meant one you'd *discovered*—one about Paolo Cafazzo. It must be why Dad went to Turkey. It must have something to do with the whole art-smuggling, art-fraud thing in the newspaper."

Ned looked as if Hazel had hit him. "Do you mean"—his voice came out in a squeak—"do you mean that it's *my* fault Dad's in trouble? It's my fault he's in jail?"

Hazel was about to say something reassuring (she just wasn't sure what) when Frankie's computer chirped. Both the children turned automatically to see who had sent the message. Hazel couldn't help herself. She gasped. It was from Oliver Frump.

With impatient fingers she reached over Ned's shoulder to click on the email. Together they read:

Dear Ned & Hazel,

Delighted to hear you can come for a visit. I have taken the liberty of booking two first-class sleeper-car tickets on the overnight train to Frontenac. It departs Friday at 10 P.M.—you may collect your tickets 45 minutes before departure from the first-class lounge. You will arrive in Frontenac at 7 o'clock on Saturday morning. A car will collect you from the station and bring you across on the ferry. Don't worry about payment; I have taken care of everything.

Please let me know by telephone or email if these arrangements are not suitable. Otherwise, I shall look forward to greeting you at Land's End tomorrow morning.

Yours truly,
Oliver Frump

Swinging her legs over the side of the bunk, Hazel contemplated the small closet where Monsieur Gentil had stowed their bags. They were traveling light: some clothing, Ned's stink bomb, and—wrapped in tissue at the bottom of the battered suitcase Monsieur Gentil had lent her—the mysterious painting by Paolo Cafazzo.

Thinking of Monsieur Gentil, Hazel smiled. After they had filled him in on everything, the old man had insisted on accompanying them, first to the station to ensure they had no difficulty collecting their tickets, and then right onto the train, just in case Richard C. Plevit or Clive Pritchard was lurking on the platform. The conductor recognized Monsieur Gentil from his own visits to the renowned café. "If they were *my* grandchildren traveling alone, I'd want to see them safely aboard too."

Hazel had been sure her brother would correct him. But Ned had simply taken the arm of his old friend and smiled his thanks to the conductor.

It hadn't been easy to fall asleep on the train, at least not at first. There was a lot to talk about, and with Ned on the top bunk (Hazel was beginning to suspect his luck with coin tosses) and Hazel below, the two chatted until well past midnight. But the endless rounds of questions neither of them could answer proved exhausting. Eventually Ned, and shortly afterward Hazel, succumbed to the combination of a long and tiring day and the soporific swaying of the train.

Now the pale light of the early-morning sun illuminated the sleeping compartment. Hazel wondered how Ned could still be asleep when there was so much to think about. Their father was still missing, locked in some prison in Istanbul, and the menacing Richard C. Plevit was still on the loose, not to mention his accomplice, Clive Pritchard. She and Ned were on their way to stay with an uncle they knew nothing about, save the fact that their father had kept his very existence a secret all their lives. And in just a few hours they'd be able to question Oliver about their father, their mother, and their past.

From the top bunk, Ned gave an enormous yawn.

He peered over the edge. "You awake, Hazel?"

"You can see I'm sitting up."

Through the window Hazel and Ned could see the passing countryside. It was as if they'd gone back in time. Fields of corn and soybeans alternated with apple orchards and the occasional pasture dotted with grazing cows. In the distance they could glimpse the shimmering blue of the lake.

"Do you think he lives on a farm?" Ned asked.

"Who? Uncle Oliver? Maybe. I was sort of picturing a small town, but I don't know anything more about Île du Loup than you do."

"I hope he's nice."

But Ned didn't sound worried. He wasn't polishing his glasses, either.

"Hey, Hazel! You didn't have that nightmare last night!" Ned said. "Do you think that's a sign?"

Hazel rolled her eyes. "Don't be ridiculous," was all she said. But privately, she couldn't help thinking maybe Ned was right.

An early breakfast was being served in the dining car before they arrived at Frontenac. Over freshly squeezed orange juice and cold toast, the children rehashed their discussion of the night before. What would Land's End be like? Could they continue to search for clues to Colin Frump's disappearance and imprisonment? Would Oliver Frump be able to explain why his brother had given Hazel that painting? Would they ever have to see Richard C. Plevit or Clive Pritchard again? Monsieur Gentil had promised to check for telephone messages from Frankie and to call them that evening.

After they had finished breakfast, Ned produced a pen and small pad of paper from the knapsack he carried with him.

"What's that for?" Hazel asked.

"We need to adopt a more rigorous approach to problem solving," Ned said sternly. "We need a more scientific method. If only to make sure that *you* don't keep forgetting things. Valuable-information-type things, like emails from long-lost uncles, for example."

Hazel stared at Ned's bent head as he jotted his notes. It *was* a good idea, but that didn't mean she had to actually say so. Ned put the pen down with a flourish and pushed the paper toward her, raising one eyebrow. "So, have I left out anything?"

Hazel scanned Ned's list quickly:

Richard C. Plevit
Clive Pritchard
Paolo Cafazzo
Inspector O'Toole
Colin Frump

art smuggling
fraud
Istanbul

"I was thinking," Ned continued, "that maybe I should add *Ludwig Barta*. I mean, he seemed nice, but it was kind of fishy, that Plevit guy showing up at his office. What if Barta left the room just so he could call Plevit and tip him off that we were there?"

"I don't think Mr. Barta had time to tip anyone off about anything," Hazel said. "But Dad did meet with him just before he disappeared, so maybe he's involved somehow. . . . Sure, put Barta's name down."

"Okay," Ned agreed, taking up the pen again, "and I think I'll add *disappearing websites* to the list too."

"Also—what was the style? *Romanticism*," Hazel added, warming to the task. "Can you remember anything else from the internet that might be helpful?"

"Like what?" Ned asked, pen poised above the paper.

Hazel shrugged. What *did* she mean?

"Like . . . other names, I guess," she said finally. "Art experts you quoted in your project."

Ned nodded. "Maybe we can track them down some other way, even if the websites aren't working."

He thought for a moment, then added:

Professor Levi Triccar
Dr. Chip Vilecart
Critic Reva L., Ph.D.

"Those are some weird names," Hazel observed. "What's with this Reva L. person? Doesn't she have a last name?"

Ned shook his head. "Nope. But it may be sort of a net name. Reva L. turned up in a lot of places. I think she must be one of those internet junkies, you know, with her own sites and chat rooms and probably more than one blog."

Hazel nodded.

"Well, that's all *I* can remember. Are you sure there's nothing else *you* remember?"

"I never saw the websites," Hazel replied.

"No, I mean stuff from when you went snooping in Dad's study, before everything got stolen," Ned answered.

Hazel shook her head. "There were just a lot of paintings and papers that I didn't get a chance to look at," she said, "and then when I came back, they were gone. Oh! Wait!"

Ned peered owlishly at her.

"Paper! I tore some pages off a notepad Dad kept beside his phone—they were all covered in doodles and scribbles."

"Well? What did they say?"

"I never looked at them again," Hazel said. "I was in such a hurry. I figured I'd do it later, but there's just been so much going on. . . ."

"Where. Are. The. Papers. Now?" Ned asked, gnashing his teeth.

Hazel couldn't remember doing anything with the scraps. Were they in her room? Did she have them at Frankie's? Where had she put those pieces of paper?

"Okay." Ned gave a theatrical, long-suffering sigh. "Think about it. You're in Dad's office. You see this notepad. You tear off some pages and you put them . . . where?"

Hazel closed her eyes. "In my pocket. My jeans pocket." Hazel dug into her pocket and pulled out several crumpled scraps of paper.

"Whoa!" Ned exclaimed. "Good thing you don't do laundry that often."

Hazel was too excited to think of a withering reply. She smoothed the papers out on the table so that they could both examine them.

The bad news was that Colin Frump's writing was almost illegible. The good news was that some of the scribbles looked remarkably like the names Ned had just written down.

"Hey! Does that say *Levi Triccar*?" Ned asked.

Hazel nodded. "And I think that must be *Critic*

Reva L.," she added. "I'm not sure about this bit at the bottom of the page. . . . Does that say 'Call S?'"

They had agreed one of the scribbles resembled the name *Clive Pritchard* and another seemed to spell *Richard C. Plevit*, but were puzzling over the others when they were interrupted.

"Are you two finished?" The waiter was hovering at Hazel's elbow. "I don't mean to rush you, but we'll be arriving at Frontenac soon."

The train was indeed slowing down. Hazel darted a quick look out the window. The farmers' fields had given way to rambling gray limestone houses and gardens overflowing with roses and hollyhocks. It was charming in a peaceful, sleepy way, she thought. It seemed . . . safe.

"Thank you," Hazel said, grabbing Ned's arm and pulling him to his feet.

The Frontenac train station was worlds removed from the one Monsieur Gentil had escorted them through the night before. There, Hazel had felt as if she was in a sort of giant cathedral, one that demanded passengers stop to admire its vaulted ceilings, soaring windows, and ornately carved stone walls. Here, the train simply halted outdoors beside a small platform and a tiny brick building decorated with gingerbread trim.

Hazel had been nervous about finding the car their

uncle had mentioned, but Ned spotted their driver almost immediately. She was tall, with tanned, freckled skin and long brown hair pulled back into a ponytail. She held a hand-lettered sign that read: FRUMPS. When Ned waved, she waved back immediately and began walking toward them.

"Hello, I'm Charlotte," she called. "Olly sent me to pick you up. Is that all you have? Just the one suitcase and your backpacks? Goodness, I know Oliver's hoping you'll stay for more than a couple of days."

Hazel shot a glance at Ned. Charlotte must be more than a hired driver—perhaps a friend?

"I think if our uncle wants us to stay longer, we probably could," Ned answered.

"Your uncle? Oh, I'm sure he'd go along with that," Charlotte said, hoisting the suitcase into the back of an old and somewhat dented blue pickup truck.

Hazel hesitated. Why had Charlotte said "your uncle" like that? Something seemed . . . not quite right. But before she could put her finger on it, Ned had pushed past her and scrambled into the cab of the truck. Charlotte was still holding the door open, her eyes fixed on Hazel with a look Hazel couldn't decipher. Were those *tears* in the woman's eyes? Just what, exactly, was going on here?

"Climb on up, Hazel," Charlotte was saying. "I'm afraid my van isn't working, so I had to bring the truck. It'll get us to Land's End just as safely. But it's not quite as comfortable. We'll have to get our air-conditioning the old-fashioned way." She pointed to the truck's open windows.

Hazel managed a thin smile in response as she climbed in beside Ned.

The drive to the ferry took no more than five minutes. As she steered the truck through the winding streets of Frontenac, Charlotte told them a little about Île du Loup.

"It's not a very big island, and it's made up mostly of farms. The ferry will take us to O'Connor's Corners, but that's nothing more than a marina, a church, and a gas station. The only real shopping is in Ville St-Pierre, on the opposite side of the island— right near Land's End, in fact. But it's geared more to the American tourists who come across the border by boat. You know: cafés, antique shops, galleries, that sort of thing. Locals generally take the ferry across to Frontenac for their shopping. . . . And here we are at the docks."

They had arrived just in time to see the island passengers disembarking.

"So how do you know our uncle Oliver?" Ned asked.

Charlotte glanced at Ned, shifting the truck into gear as the ferryman waved the car ahead of her onto the boat. When she had steered the truck into place, she switched off the ignition and paused, her hand still resting on the keys.

"How long have I known . . . *who*?" she asked.

"Uncle Oliver," Ned repeated.

"You mean Uncle *Seamus*," Charlotte corrected.

"No, he means our uncle Oliver," Hazel said. She could feel a knot forming in her stomach. "Oliver Frump. Our father, Colin Frump, is his brother. You're supposed to be taking us to Oliver." Despite her best efforts, Hazel's voice wobbled slightly.

"It's okay," Charlotte said soothingly. "I *am* taking you to Oliver."

"Then who's Seamus?" asked Ned.

Charlotte paused. "You know what? I think Oliver should explain that," she said. "Now, if you'll excuse me, I have to go see a man about a horse."

"I beg your pardon?" Hazel asked.

"Did I mention I'm a vet? That fine gentleman over there could use a gentle reminder about paying my last bill," Charlotte said. "Why don't you two stretch your legs, enjoy the fresh air—just meet me back here before we dock."

With that, she was gone. Hazel and Ned looked at each other. Ned shrugged.

"Let's go see what there is to see," he suggested without enthusiasm. They clambered out of the truck and made for one of the narrow metal staircases that led to the decks where passengers, soaked in spray, leaned over the rails and chatted as they surveyed the circling gulls and the few sailboats hardy enough to brave the choppy waters.

But as they reached the deck, a scuffle broke out below them. Turning, Hazel and Ned saw two fair-haired boys, roughly Hazel's age, trying to break free from one of the ferrymen. The man had one of the boys by the ear and the other by the neck of his T-shirt. A taller boy with dark curly hair was hanging back, watching the scene with narrowed eyes. Hazel felt her eyes drawn to him.

"You think soaping the windows of people's cars is funny?" bellowed the ferryman. "Let's just see how funny you think it is to clean it off, then!"

"It wasn't us," whined the larger of the blond kids. He had stopped trying to get away; his shoulders slumped in defeat.

"No? Then what're you doin' with this, mister?" the ferryman demanded, thrusting a bar of soap under the boy's chin.

Hazel could see that two of the cars parked below had rude words written on their rear windows.

"He was trying to wash my mouth out with soap," giggled the smaller boy. The bigger boy scowled at him before turning to the dark-haired boy.

"C'mon, Hank, tell him it wasn't us," he whined.

Hank. Now there's an old-fashioned, country sort of name, Hazel thought. Someone named Hank just had to be a baseball player, she decided, not a hockey player, and definitely not a basketball player.

Hazel hadn't realized she was staring until Hank looked straight at her. Their eyes locked for a moment. Then Hazel looked away.

"You're on your own, Billy," Hank said in a careless tone. "I was watching a bird. I don't know what you two were up to."

Hazel steered Ned toward the far side of the boat. When she glanced casually back, Hank was gone.

"What do you think Charlotte meant about 'Uncle Seamus'?" Ned asked. "Do you think there's a whole bunch of uncles we don't know about?"

"At this point, nothing would surprise me," Hazel replied. "Maybe there're aunts, too."

"And cousins."

"Well, we'll find out for ourselves soon enough—there's the dock, over there."

As they started to make their way back to Charlotte's truck, Hazel scanned the crowd for the boy called Hank. She caught sight of him over by a gleaming black pickup truck parked at the front of the ferry, the two other boys beside him. The ferryman was there too, arguing with the driver of the truck—a slim man in jeans and a T-shirt, with blond hair peeking out below his cap. A pair of sunglasses shielded his eyes.

"I wonder if that's their dad," Hazel murmured.

As she strained to get a better look at the man, he turned. Hazel caught a glimpse of his face. She let out a squeak and pinched Ned, hard.

"Ow!" her brother yelped. "What's the matter with you?"

A middle-aged woman glanced up from her newspaper, curious, but Hazel ignored her. Putting a finger to her lips, she grabbed Ned's arm and pulled him behind a gaggle of chattering teenagers. Her heart was beating wildly.

"You're freaking me out," whispered Ned, but his voice was calm.

"Did you see? Did you see the man with those boys—that Hank guy and the other two?" hissed Hazel, peering around the corner.

"What man?" demanded Ned.

"There, with the sunglasses—getting into the pickup truck." Hazel pointed. "It's, you know, Ferrari Guy—whatsisname—the one the newspaper said was Dad's partner. It's Clive Pritchard!"

The black pickup was the first vehicle to drive off the ferry. The children drew back slightly as it passed. The three boys were sitting in the cab; the back of the truck was covered with a tarpaulin that had come untied at one corner. Hazel glimpsed a stack of packages wrapped in brown paper.

They were slim and flat—like paintings ready for shipping.

"Hey, Frumps!" It was Charlotte, beckoning them to the blue truck.

"We'll talk about it later?" Hazel whispered. Ned nodded.

"We're coming!" the children called.

The drive to Land's End took about half an hour and passed by nearly a hundred farms. No one spoke until they crested a long hill that opened up a postcard vista of the lake, with dozens of sailboats and a couple of larger vessels that looked like passenger ferries.

"What are those?" Hazel asked, pointing.

"This is where Lake Ontario meets the Saint Lawrence River," Charlotte explained. "Those are tour boats that take Canadian and American tourists to the area called the Thousand Islands. They circle around Île du Loup on their way out, because we're so 'picturesque.'"

As they drove on down into Ville St-Pierre, Hazel could see it was bigger than O'Connor's Corners, where the ferry had docked. But it was still, as Ned put it, "no thriving metropolis." Hazel noticed a greengrocer's, a general store, a butcher's shop, a repair shop, half a dozen antique shops, and a café with a sign that read: ART, TEAS, BOOKS, AND ANTIQUES. There was no sign of Clive Pritchard.

Just beyond the village, Charlotte stopped the truck. They were at the entrance to a long, winding driveway flanked by spreading maple trees. On one side of the driveway sprawled an old apple orchard, on the other a rolling expanse of lawn. But it was the house that amazed both of them.

It was bigger than the biggest mansion Hazel had ever seen—more the size of a large school—and built of rough-hewn stone, overgrown in places by ivy. The gray walls were punctuated at odd intervals by tall, arched windows, and Hazel counted three round towers. Two had conical slate roofs, but one was open at the top, perhaps to serve as a lookout over the lake. The walls of that tower alternated between high and low sections. There was a word for that, Hazel knew, but she couldn't remember it.

"Battlements!" Ned breathed. "An actual castle with actual battlements."

Hazel wondered what sort of battle the castle's owners might have waged. It looked awfully familiar. Could she have seen it before? She glanced at Ned; his mouth had fallen open. She turned to look at Charlotte.

"It sure is something," Charlotte agreed, putting

the truck in gear again and heading slowly up the drive. "People around here call it The Folly. Your family always calls it Land's End, though. This road is Land's End Lane. I think your cousins consider the word *folly* a bit hard-hearted.

"Still, it was a crazy project. It was built more than a hundred years ago by a French immigrant for his Irish wife. It's meant to combine elements of a castle near her home in the south of Ireland with one near his home in the north of France. It makes for an unusual collaboration of architectural styles, I suppose you'd say. . . . He died before he could finish it."

"I feel like I've seen this place before," Ned said in a strangled voice. Hazel was about to ask him where, when it hit her: This was the castle from the painting. This was Paolo Cafazzo's castle!

Hazel stared. This castle had to be the one from the painting! Except . . . something wasn't quite right. Maybe it was the angle, the view from the truck. As she puzzled over it, the pickup reached the top of a small rise, giving Hazel her first glimpse of the lake beyond the castle. She caught her breath. A fat stone tower was clearly visible some distance behind and to the left of Land's End. Hazel couldn't take her eyes off it. She *knew* that tower. And not from a painting.

"What's that place?" she asked. "I can't see it very well from here, but it looks too far away to be part of Land's End."

Charlotte nodded. "That's a Martello tower," she said. "It's on a little island just behind Land's End. There are a few towers like that around Frontenac, left over from the days when they were needed to help guard the town and the port. Some have been turned into museums, but not that one. It's sort of . . . abandoned, I guess. A few of the villagers say it's haunted."

Hazel shivered. Charlotte looked at her in some amusement.

"You don't believe in ghosts, do you?" Charlotte asked.

Before Hazel could answer, a loud beeping noise pierced the air. Charlotte braked, reached into her purse, and pulled out a pager.

"Oh, heck—Carol Jupiter's horse is in trouble again! I've got to dash. Do you kids mind if I drop you here? You can tell Oliver I said hi, and that I'll come by later to discuss . . . er, your visit with your uncle."

"Sure," Hazel said faintly. "No problem."

As the blue pickup sped down the road, Ned gripped Hazel's arm so tightly, she winced.

"Hazel, do you realize where we are?" Ned asked. "This is the castle. *The* castle—the one in Paolo Cafazzo's painting!"

Hazel nodded. But she was still thinking about the tower. It wasn't in the painting. So why did it seem so familiar?

Ned was still talking. "And of course, this has to mean Uncle Oliver's loaded too, just like Dad." He frowned. "Or maybe he isn't, Hazel. I mean, maybe

Dad got all the Frump money and Uncle Oliver got the castle. I think if it was me, I'd rather have the castle."

Ned was still pondering the pros and cons of fortresses versus fortunes when they reached the end of the long driveway and stood, hesitating, in the shadow of the castle. They were wondering whether they should climb the stone steps to the great wooden door, or if there might be a less forbidding entrance somewhere, when a small boy skidded around the corner and stopped in front of them.

"You made it! You made it!"

Hazel caught her breath. The boy had ruler-straight dark brown hair and glasses. He was almost the same height and weight as Ned, perhaps an inch shorter. The resemblance was uncanny.

"You must be Ned," the boy said, holding out his hand.

"Yeah," Ned confirmed, shaking hands a bit stiffly.

"And you must be Hazel." The boy turned to smile up at her before pumping her arm energetically.

She nodded and returned the smile, wondering when he would introduce himself.

"I'm . . . I'm pleased to meet you," the boy said after a slight pause. "Welcome to Land's End or, as they say in the village, The Folly."

"Thanks. Who are you?" Ned asked bluntly. "And where's our uncle Oliver?"

"I'm . . . I'm your cousin, of course," the boy stammered. "Come on up—we should let Deirdre know you're here."

With that, the boy turned and led the way up the short flight of broad stone steps to the veranda. The castle was girded by a stone terrace. It was covered by a flat roof, which created a covered area below and an open one above. This lower level felt far too grand to be called a porch, but that was clearly how Uncle Oliver treated it. Books and games were scattered about on wicker chairs, and a basket was jammed full of tennis rackets and baseball bats. There was even a porch swing.

"Wait! Who's Deirdre?" Ned asked. But the boy had run ahead and either couldn't hear him or didn't want to answer.

"Deirdre—our visitors are here!" the boy yelled.

A wooden screen door at the far end of the porch opened, and a sandy-haired girl in shorts and a faded T-shirt stepped out. In her arms she cradled a copper bowl filled with peas still in their pods. She was the same height as Hazel but appeared to be older, although that might have been due to the intimidating scowl on her face.

"Oliver, what are you talking about?" the girl asked. "You're supposed to be helping me shell the peas! What do you mean, visitors?"

But when she saw Hazel and Ned, she stopped dead in her tracks.

"Oh. I . . . omigosh . . ." Her voice trailed off as she stared at them. She wasn't frowning now; she looked as if she'd seen a ghost. The bowl slipped out of her hands and clattered to the floor below, pods scattering across the flagstones.

"Oh my. Oh my goodness. You're . . . you're Hazel and N-Ned," she stammered.

Hazel and Ned exchanged glances.

"Yes, I'm Hazel, and this is my brother, Ned," Hazel began slowly. "But we're a little confused. We came to visit our uncle Oliver."

The girl turned to the younger boy, who was now perched on the porch swing, grinning nervously.

"Oliver! What have you done?"

"Wait a minute. *You're* Uncle Oliver?" Ned pointed an accusing finger at the boy.

"What's going on?" Hazel appealed to the older girl.

"That's what I'd like to know," she said, turning to the boy. "But it looks like my brother's the only one who can answer that. Well, Oliver?"

"They called—I mean . . . he called. . . . Ned," Oliver replied. "I think he must have been looking for Dad, but somehow he had my name instead. He said they wanted to come and visit. So I said sure. Don't be

123

mad, Deirdre. It's what we've always wanted."

"I did call," Ned agreed. "And I did ask for Oliver. I thought that was our uncle's name."

"Nope. Our dad's name is Seamus; *I'm* Oliver," the boy explained. "But when I got your message, I figured you might not come if you knew it was just me."

No wonder Charlotte had decided to make Oliver explain. But why hadn't Frankie set them straight? Hazel thought back to their hurried phone conversation. Frankie had said their father had a brother, but she had never actually called him Oliver. In fact, hadn't she said Oliver didn't sound right?

"I thought . . . I mean, I found an email to my Dad from an Oliver Frump, about a family reunion," Hazel said. "And then we found out that there was a brother. I mean, an uncle. So I guess we just assumed— I assumed—that the uncle was named Oliver. We didn't know there were any other relatives. . . ."

"A classic case of two plus two equaling five," Ned observed, shaking his head.

"Wait a second. You emailed Uncle Colin?" Deirdre's hands were on her hips. She glared at Oliver. "Oh, you are so busted. Wait until Dad finds out."

Deirdre turned back toward Hazel. Her blue eyes no longer blazed with indignation. Now they were just bewildered.

"But how did you get here?" she asked, looking

from Hazel to Ned and back again. "I mean, Oliver's right. We've all wanted you to come for ages, but now you suddenly show up. It's like magic."

"There's nothing very magical about booking train tickets online and asking Charlotte to pick them up at the train station and bring 'em over on the ferry," Oliver said.

"*You* did all that?" asked Ned in tones of begrudging admiration.

"I hope you used some kind of magic to pay for everything," Deirdre said. "Considering that the last time Dad found out you'd used his credit card to buy something over the internet, he flipped out."

"Look, if there's a problem, we can pay you back," Hazel said. An uncomfortable feeling was growing in the pit of her stomach. She felt as if she had arrived at a party only to find her invitation had been issued by mistake.

"Gosh no, I'm sorry. There's no problem," Deirdre said quickly. "I'm really glad you guys came. *Everybody's* going to be glad."

"Everybody?" asked Hazel. "Who is everybody?"

Deirdre slipped an arm around Hazel's shoulders and guided her to a wicker love seat, motioning to Ned to follow. She plunked herself down on the footstool facing them.

"Okay, here's the thing," Deirdre said, taking a deep

breath. "My name's Deirdre, and I'm your cousin. I'm fourteen. Oliver is eight. Then there are our older brothers, Matthew and Mark. They're seventeen. They're twins and they're adopted. Their dad was from Montreal and their mom was from Trinidad, but their biological parents died a long time ago."

"But there is an uncle, too, right? Uncle Seamus? You're not orphans, right?" Hazel asked.

Deirdre blinked.

"Oh, no! I mean yes. I mean no, we're not orphans, and, yes, there is an uncle." Deirdre shook her head like a swimmer trying to empty water from her ears. "Our father—your father's brother—is Seamus: Seamus Frump."

"Got it," Hazel said.

"So I guess you don't remember . . . I mean, I guess you two don't really know anything about us, huh?" Deirdre asked softly.

Hazel shook her head. Her brain was spinning. How could their father have hidden all these relatives from them? Why would he keep them a secret?

"Nope. We've never heard of any of you," Ned said. "You didn't mention an aunt. Is there one?"

Deirdre flicked a glance at Oliver and cleared her throat.

"No," she said reluctantly. "Our mother died when I was six years old."

126

"Oh. Sorry," Ned said. "Our mother's dead too. She died when I was a baby."

"I know," Deirdre murmured.

For a few moments nobody spoke. Hazel suddenly felt very tired. She was vividly aware of how soft the cushion on the love seat felt and how nearby pale-yellow roses, climbing a trellis they had overgrown, were filling the air with a heavy perfume. She could hear bees humming in the vines and the singing of a cicada. She heard Ned's stomach growl.

"So, where *is* Uncle Seamus?" Ned asked. "Does he even know we're coming?"

The boy Oliver shook his head. Deirdre grimaced.

"Well, that should be the first topic for discussion once the twins get back from sailing," she said. "Dad's away, and he's actually not due back for days, maybe even weeks. I'm sure once he hears about you two, he's going to want to come home as soon as possible, so we'll have to decide when to break the news."

"Where is he?" Hazel asked.

"He's in Ottawa, trying a case before the Supreme Court," Deirdre said. Hazel thought she detected a note of pride in her cousin's voice.

"He's a lawyer?" Hazel asked.

"A really good one." Deirdre's pride was undisguised now.

"Well, that could come in handy," Ned muttered.

Hazel jammed an elbow into his ribs.

"I beg your pardon?" Deirdre asked.

"Uh, got any candy?" Ned asked. "I'm starved."

"Oh goodness, where are our manners?" Deirdre said. She turned to Oliver. "Take your cousin inside and find him a snack! Or better yet, why don't you boys get started on lunch? Hazel and I will come and help in a few minutes."

Deirdre was a little bossy, Hazel reflected. But as long as the bossiness was directed at someone other than her, she wouldn't protest. Hazel nodded to Ned.

"We'll be right behind you," she told him. "Don't do anything I wouldn't do."

She hoped Ned would take the hint and keep quiet about Colin Frump's imprisonment. Uncle Seamus might be just the person they needed right now, but until they found out more about why he and their dad didn't speak to each other, Hazel didn't know if they could trust him. Ned nodded and slid off the love seat.

"After lunch, want to see my room?" Oliver asked. "I have the coolest chemistry set you've ever seen."

"Oh, I really doubt that," Ned replied. "But sure, I'll check it out."

As the screen door slammed behind the boys, Hazel turned to Deirdre. "So . . . it can't have been easy growing up as the only girl in a house with three brothers. It's too bad we didn't have each other to talk to, all these years."

"Uh-huh. Want to go for a walk along the beach, or take a tour of the castle?" Deirdre asked brightly.

"Sure. I'm dying to see the rest of the castle," Hazel said, smiling back at the older girl.

Stepping over the scattered peas, Deirdre opened the screen door and led Hazel through the largest kitchen she had ever seen. Monsieur Gentil would flip if he ever saw it. The room was so long and wide that there was space for tables, bookcases, and armchairs, as well as fitted cupboards and counters. The flagstone floor was worn smooth in front of the old-fashioned iron stove. Next to the stove stood an enormous fireplace, with a hearth opening so tall that Oliver was demonstrating to Ned how he could walk right into the chimney. Hazel fell in love with the place instantly.

But Deirdre was already ushering her into the hall, where the ceilings were high enough that Hazel was pretty sure you could attach NBA regulation-height hoops to most of the stone or wood-paneled walls, and still have loads of room to spare. There was a full suit of armor standing at attention, and Hazel desperately wanted to sneak a peek behind its visor, but Deirdre was setting a brisk pace. There were so many rooms and hallways, it was impossible to fix them all in her memory. There was an actual ballroom in the main part of the building, and in one of the towers Hazel was thrilled to see a two-story library. It was a completely round room, lined from floor to ceiling with books. A narrow circular staircase led to an equally narrow balcony that encircled the room. Hazel itched to climb the stairs and examine the upper tiers of books, but Deirdre was already pulling her into another corridor.

Hazel had lost count of living rooms, parlors, game rooms, and bedrooms by the time Deirdre led her through a rounded oak door into a courtyard.

"Cloisters!" exclaimed Hazel. "I thought that was something you only found in churches or monasteries!"

"Land's End has almost everything you can imagine." Deirdre laughed. "Except a swimming pool; with the lake right outside, you don't really need one. You haven't seen the best thing yet. Come on!"

She pulled Hazel through another door. This one led directly to a small, circular stone staircase, which Deirdre climbed, two steps at a time. When they reached the top, Deirdre was out of breath and needed Hazel's help to push open the trapdoor.

"Wow," breathed Hazel as the girls scrambled out into the sunshine. They were standing atop the open tower with the battlements. Hazel's stomach was turning flip-flops and her head felt light and woozy; her successful escape from the museum had done nothing to lessen her fear of heights. She stayed a few paces behind her cousin as Deirdre moved closer to the crenellated wall that encircled the platform. Up here the breeze was stronger, more like wind, and the girls' hair was blowing around their faces. But when Hazel pulled her hair back and gazed at the glittering lake, she had to admit the view was spectacular. Terrifying, but spectacular.

"This tower is actually taller than the others," Deirdre pointed out. "The northwest tower is where the boys' rooms are, and the southwest tower is where my room is, and Dad's room, and a guest room—you can have that one tonight, if you like. Anyway, we don't really know why this tower doesn't have a roof like the others, but if you ask me, it does have the best view. I think the fourth tower was going to be like this one, with an open lookout. But I'm kind of glad they never finished that one; it makes this one more special, even though it does ruin the symmetry.

"From here you can see that the castle is built on a sort of peninsula. Beyond the orchard and the hill, there's an even better beach, with sand dunes and the whitest, softest sand. And way, way beyond *that*, there's a really interesting old lighthouse. It hasn't been used to warn ships in almost a century, but it's still standing. We'll take you there for a picnic or a midnight bonfire some night. Oh—and we have the greatest tree fort you've ever seen. It's really, really old, and stretches between three different trees!"

Deirdre's eyes were shining.

"Please," Hazel said, putting her hand on Deirdre's arm. "I don't mean to be rude. But . . . this is so strange for me. You and Oliver know all about me and Ned, and you're talking about picnics and bonfires and stuff. But we just met you! We didn't know you even existed until today!"

Deirdre looked uncomfortably at Hazel. "I'm not the right person to explain it all."

"But why didn't my dad ever tell us about your dad? Did they have a big fight or something?" asked Hazel.

Deirdre winced. "You see . . . it's a whole big, complicated thing, and I'd just mess it up. I mean, I'd leave out stuff or I'd get it wrong. And it's important that you hear the whole story—from the right person."

Deirdre paused. She seemed to be choosing her words carefully. "*Our* father never kept you two a secret," she said finally. "So, yeah, we know your names, and how old you are, and there are a few old photographs around."

She paused again. When she resumed, her voice sounded strained. "But you have to believe me when I say that I can't explain why your dad never told you about us, or why we've never met. You just have to wait for Dad."

"But . . . does our father know you guys live in a castle?" Hazel asked. "Because I just can't believe he would've kept this place a secret."

"Does he know?" Deirdre echoed. "Well, yeah—he was born here. They both were—our dads, I mean. They're twins. I guess I didn't mention that. Identical twins, not fraternal, like Matt and Mark, but not, like, freaky identical. I think if they were standing together, you could tell them apart. But if you only had one in front of you, it might take you a minute to figure out which one he was."

Hazel's mind was spinning. Her father had an identical twin? How could she not know something like that? How could he not have told her? And how could he not have told her he'd grown up in a castle?

"I wonder if my mom knew that Dad had a twin," Hazel said. "I wonder if he ever told *her* about this place."

"Don't ask me," Deirdre replied.

Her voice sounded odd, Hazel thought. This family, she decided, was insane. When she grew up, if she had kids, she'd tell them everything—*everything*—even stuff they didn't want to hear.

Deirdre was studying her with a worried look. "Oh, Hazel, don't let it drive you nuts. Please? We're so happy to have you guys here. We've wanted to see you for ages. I'd never let on to Oliver, but I think he's done everyone a big favor. In the meantime, we should take advantage of our fathers not being here and just . . . have a blast. You know?"

Hazel sighed. Okay. If Deirdre wouldn't confide in her, she wouldn't confide in Deirdre—at least not yet. Maybe one of the other cousins would be willing to talk. Meanwhile, she might as well steer Deirdre toward happier subjects.

"So . . . Matthew and Mark aren't identical twins?" she asked.

Deirdre's face relaxed. "No, no. Matt and Mark don't look alike at all. And they *hate* being compared to each other, so of course Oliver and I do that all the time. But they get along really well. With each other, I mean. They're starting university this fall, but they'll be going to different schools."

Looking past Deirdre, beyond the parapet, Hazel gazed out toward the island with the Martello tower. Deirdre hadn't mentioned that tower when she was pointing out the scenery. Why not?

"Does somebody own that island?" Hazel asked, gesturing toward it.

"Hmm? Oh, we do, but I haven't been there in years."

"I'd like to go see it sometime," Hazel said.

"Oh no, no, no," Deirdre said, shaking her head. Her voice sounded a little shaky too, Hazel thought. "That tower's falling apart and the island is pretty small, and it's not like there's anything to *do* there."

Deirdre took Hazel's arm as if to steer her away from the sight of the tower. Was it Hazel's imagination, or had Deirdre turned a little pale?

"I mean, the current's much too strong to swim over there, and even if you took a boat, well, pretty much the whole place is covered in poison ivy. Some kids even say the tower's haunted. Of course that's silly, but still, I mean, why take chances?"

Hazel was staring at the tower with narrowed eyes. There was a man leaning out of one of the tower windows. He was too far away to get a good look, but she had the grim feeling that his bulky frame and bald head were horribly familiar. Her heart slammed against her ribs.

"Do you see that man?" Hazel asked.

Deirdre turned to look. "Where?"

"Just there, in the window!" But the man had drawn his head back inside the tower.

"No one's there," Deirdre announced. "Anyway, Mark and Matt must be home by now. Aren't you dying to meet them?"

Hazel nodded, although for now she didn't care the slightest bit about meeting her cousins. She just wanted to warn Ned that Clive Pritchard wasn't the only man they had to worry about on Île du Loup.

Richard C. Plevit was here too.

9

"**H**ey, Hazel—come and meet Matt and Mark! Oliver calls 'em the M&M's—you know, like the candy!"

Ned was sitting beside Oliver on the porch swing. For one disconcerting second, Hazel wasn't sure which boy was which. Ned seemed different somehow. He looked completely relaxed. He's really hit it off with Oliver, Hazel thought as the younger boy whispered something in Ned's ear that set the pair of them giggling like crazy. Mark and Matthew were leaning against the stone balustrade, surveying the younger boys with amused expressions.

This was all very cozy, but Hazel needed to get Ned to herself, to tell him about seeing Richard C. Plevit in the tower. Unless she wanted to share the news with everyone . . . but they'd probably think she was nuts. Or making it up.

"Hi, Hazel. I'm Matt," said the shorter of the twins.

They were definitely not identical; Hazel wouldn't even have known the teenagers were twins if Deirdre hadn't told her. Matt had a stockier build, lighter skin, and close-cropped hair. He wore a sober expression that seemed to suit his plain jeans and white polo shirt. Mark's skin was very dark, and he was at least six inches taller than his twin, but looked as if he weighed considerably less. He wore his hair in cornrows and had a pair of tinted glasses perched at the end of his nose. His Hawaiian shirt was unbuttoned, revealing a tattered T-shirt that read: DANDELIONS DON'T CAUSE CANCER—LAWN CHEMICALS DO.

"Hi," Hazel said, but that was as far as she got before Mark lifted her off her feet in a giant bear hug and twirled her around.

"Hey, little cousin—long time no see!" he said, setting her down gently. "Ned was just telling us you guys might stay for a while. That's the best news we've had in a long time."

Hazel stared at her cousin. Mark might be skinny, but he sure was strong. Hazel was tall for her age and, thanks to all those hours on the basketball court, she had muscles, too. She was *solid*. People didn't just go around picking her up like she was a little kid.

"We're all very happy to see you," Matt said more formally. "We were just talking about the fact that we should tell our father about you two. . . . He'll be very happy too, of course. But maybe we'll just wait until he calls."

"He's supposed to check in tomorrow, right?" Deirdre asked.

Matt nodded. "The thing is, this case he's trying is a little tricky, and we don't want to do anything that would throw him off," Matt said. "I mean, we don't want to disturb him."

"Sure," Hazel agreed. That would give her a little more time to talk things over with Ned and decide how much to tell Uncle Seamus and the cousins.

"Oh—there's the phone," Deirdre said. "Oliver, you get it!"

She really is bossy, Hazel thought. Deirdre was standing much closer to the screen door than her little brother. But Oliver leaped up obediently and headed into the kitchen. He was back in a minute, holding a portable phone.

"There's some guy with a really thick French accent asking for 'Azel or Ned," Oliver announced.

"Oh, that's Monsieur Gentil, our neighbor. We left him your phone number. He probably just wants to make sure we got here okay," Hazel said. "Ned, we should talk to him."

Almost imperceptibly, Hazel jerked her head toward the kitchen door. This was her chance to get Ned away from the others.

"So give her the phone, Squirt," Deirdre ordered Oliver.

Hazel blinked: *Squirt* was what she called Ned. This was weird.

"Actually, do you mind if we take it inside?" Ned asked.

"Go ahead," Matt replied. "We'll be out here."

The conversation with Monsieur Gentil did not last long; he was in the midst of a rush of tourists from a nearby exhibition. Ned and Hazel assured the old man they were safe. He told them that a locksmith friend had already changed the locks on the door leading from the staircase to the floor where the Frumps and Frankie lived, as well as the locks on the doors to their apartments.

"And I worked a little sabotage on the elevator, myself," Monsieur Gentil said. "I will apologize to your father on his return, but in the meantime, I promise you, no one will be using it. Everyone must take the stairs. It is good for their health, *non*?"

The entrance to the staircase was right beside Monsieur Gentil's café. Now he could easily keep track of who was coming and going from the apartments.

"Thanks, Monsieur Gentil," Ned told him. "We'll be in touch."

After they had hung up, Hazel told Ned she didn't think there would have been any more disturbances at the apartment building anyway.

"Well, Ferrari Guy—I mean, Clive Pritchard—is here on the island," Ned agreed. "But don't forget about Richard C. Plevit—the one who hurt Frankie."

Ned's eyes widened as Hazel described seeing Plevit lean out of the tower.

"Do you think they're following us?" Ned asked, removing his glasses. "Should we tell the others?"

From outside came laughter and the murmured conversation of their cousins. Hazel watched Ned for a moment. His glasses were off, but he wasn't actually polishing them. Did he feel it too, she wondered? Did he feel safe?

"I don't think they're following us," Hazel answered. "Frankie said she thought Dad knew Clive Pritchard from a long time ago. I wonder if it could have been from here, from Île du Loup. Deirdre says Dad was born here, and grew up here."

"Man—how could he grow up in a castle and not tell us?" asked Ned.

"Oh, that's not all," Hazel said. "Get this. Apparently he and Uncle Seamus are identical twins."

Ned grimaced. "I've changed my mind," he announced. "Dad's not secretive; he's nuts. How could he have an identical twin *and not tell us?*"

"I'm right there with you," Hazel said. "But in the meantime, we still have to deal with Clive Pritchard and Richard C. Plevit being on the island. It's strange, but when I think about it now, I don't actually feel afraid. Even though I probably should. Isn't that weird?"

Ned nodded. "It *is* weird, but I kind of feel the same way," he replied. "I feel a bit nervous and sort of excited, I suppose. But not scared. Maybe it's just because we're better off now."

"What do you mean?" asked Hazel.

"Well . . . we're not alone anymore," Ned pointed out, "and Matt and Mark are *almost* like grown-ups, and staying in a castle just has to be better than hiding out at Frankie's and waiting for the burglars to come back. I sort of wish there was a moat, though."

Hazel grinned.

"I think we should tell them everything—they might be able to help," Ned said in a serious voice. "I think there are way too many secrets in this family."

"You're not worried they'll think we're crazy?" Hazel asked.

Deep down, she knew Ned was right—they had to come clean. Still, she'd feel better about it if she knew why Colin and Seamus were estranged. Weren't twins supposed to be closer than other brothers and sisters?

"Hey, Ned—it must have been something pretty

big that drove Dad and Uncle Seamus apart, right?"

"Maybe. Or maybe it was something little or stupid and they've been too embarrassed to call each other," Ned answered. "We've had lots of fights about stupid stuff."

"It wasn't little or stupid—I'm sure of that," Hazel said. "There's something seriously wrong here."

"But the cousins seem to know all about us, so maybe Uncle Seamus isn't angry," Ned suggested. "Maybe he's ready to make up."

"Could be . . . but it's all so weird. I tried asking Deirdre about Mom, but she clammed right up. And how strange is it that their mom died too? Two brothers, both widowers . . . you'd think that would bring our dads closer together."

Ned nodded. "Like I said, there are way too many secrets in this family. But what about the note Dad made? He wrote 'call S.' He might have meant 'call Seamus.' Maybe he was going to tell Uncle Seamus everything. Or maybe he already *did* tell him."

Hazel held her head in her hands. After a few minutes she looked up. "Okay, we'll tell the cousins everything we know. Tomorrow. Let's just give ourselves today to get to know one another."

Oliver wasn't quite as firmly under Deirdre's thumb as Hazel had thought. It turned out that as soon as the girls had embarked on their tour, the boys had grabbed a handful of cookies and headed straight for Oliver's room—a place, Ned assured Hazel, that boasted something closer to a chemistry *lab* than a simple chemistry set. Oliver was going to help Ned refine the NIDS.

"We might have to change the name to NOIDS— for Ned and Oliver's Incredibly Disgusting Stink-bomb," Ned said happily.

"Stink bomb?" Mark poked his head through the screen door. "Oh, man—are you another chemistry freak like Olly? One is bad enough!"

"What kind of stuff does Oliver invent?" Hazel said.

"Don't get me started," Mark said darkly. "Listen, you guys, we were all just talking about taking a picnic to the beach. We can throw a whole bunch of food in a basket and spend the rest of the day swimming. . . . What do you say?"

Hazel and Ned needed no persuading. Oliver promised to find Ned a spare bathing suit in the jumble of his room, and the two boys set off together. Deirdre smiled at Hazel and gestured for her to follow.

"I'm sure I've got something you can borrow, if you didn't pack a bathing suit," the older girl said. "And I'll show you the tower room where you'll be sleeping while you're here."

"Hey, be quick, you two! No trying stuff on and looking in mirrors," Mark called after them as they hurried up the stone staircase. "Time's a-wastin'! Surf's up!"

With Mark's words ringing in her ears, Hazel was determined to be the first one changed. She barely glanced at the perfectly round room that would be hers later that night, taking only seconds to pull on the bathing suit Deirdre had thrust into her hands and to stuff her unruly hair into a ponytail. But the castle's layout was confusing, and by the time Hazel had found the kitchen again, the twins had finished assembling an impressive array of sandwiches, fruit, and drinks for the picnic.

Assuming that they were just headed to the pebbly shore close by, Ned was mystified by the elaborate preparations.

"No, we're going to the real beach—the sand dunes," Oliver told him. "They're the best ones on the whole island. Come on, follow me!"

Hazel and Ned practically lived at the beach at home. But the sand there was coarse and, as often as not, littered with candy wrappers, pieces of glass, and bits of plastic. The beach at Land's End had the softest, whitest sand Hazel had ever seen. The dunes—undulating waves of sand crested with tall grasses—appeared with startling suddenness just beyond the edge of the old orchard. One minute Hazel was walking under tree boughs laden with small unripe fruit; the next, she was sliding down a steep grassy slope and gaping at the broad crescent of sand that stretched before her, and the sparkling water beyond.

The rest of the afternoon passed so peacefully, Hazel felt as if they had entered another world. She swam for a while, but the water still had that early-summer chill, and the lure of the sun and the sand proved stronger. Lazing on a beach towel, Hazel talked with Mark and Deirdre about harmless topics like boarding school, basketball, Deirdre's cross-country running championship, and Mark's difficulty in deciding between being a lawyer like Uncle Seamus or a great chef.

After hours of watching Ned and Oliver construct the most impossibly elaborate sand fortress, Hazel had almost succeeded in forgetting the events that had brought them here. At least until Matt emerged from a lengthy swim to take a seat on a nearby towel and ask, "So, what made you guys decide to come visit us, anyway?" He was sitting with the sun behind him; to look at him, Hazel had to squint and shield her eyes with her hand. She fumbled for words.

"Uh . . . well, our dad had to go out of town, and then the woman who was staying with us, she had to leave too—unexpectedly," Hazel said. She could feel her skin flushing and hoped Matt would think it was the sun. "So we decided it would be . . . more fun to come visit than to . . . you know, stay in the city by ourselves."

"The babysitter left too?" Deirdre asked in a shocked tone. "If you ask me, that's just terrible! She shouldn't have left you kids alone."

Hazel could feel the beginnings of anger stirring inside her; who said anything about a *babysitter*? And who was Deirdre to call *her* a kid when there were only two years between them?

"Actually, in this province Hazel's old enough not to need a babysitter," Mark pointed out, "legally speaking, I mean."

"Still, if the woman was being paid . . ." Deirdre began to argue.

"I didn't say she was *hired* to look after us," Hazel said frostily. "She's a friend of the family. And she had a good reason for going! It was a family emergency!"

"Oh," replied Deirdre. She smiled at Hazel. It was an apologetic smile, Hazel realized. "I'm really sorry. Dad's always telling me to stop and think before I speak," Deirdre admitted.

"It's okay." Hazel's voice was somewhat muffled. She had rolled over onto her stomach and put her head down on her towel. She wasn't upset, not really. But she needed to end this conversation before she divulged more than she wanted to.

Matt looked at his watch. "It's getting late," he

said. "Why don't we pack up, go back home, and throw some clothes on. We can take a walk into the village for some ice cream or something."

Everyone agreed. They gathered the picnic things and towels and headed back to the castle. As they climbed the steps to the porch, they could hear the telephone ringing in the kitchen. This time Deirdre was the one to grab it.

"Hello? Oh, Mr. Gentil? No, I'm Hazel and Ned's cousin. But they're right here. I'll get them for you."

Hazel caught her breath. Why was Monsieur Gentil calling back so soon? Had something happened? She stretched out a trembling hand for the phone, but Ned beat her to it.

"Hello? It's me, Ned," he said. "What's up?"

Hazel watched as her brother listened for a few minutes.

"Oh. Well, no, it wasn't," he said finally. "You can tell her if she calls again. Okay, well, thanks. We'll talk to you soon," Ned said. "'Bye."

"Everything okay?" asked Deirdre, eyes bright with curiosity.

"Sure, fine," Ned replied. But he looked at Hazel as if he wanted to say more and couldn't.

"Well, let's everybody get changed and meet back here in ten, okay?" Matt said, looking at his cousins.

The Île du Loup Frumps headed to their rooms.

Alone at last in the kitchen, Ned gazed worriedly at Hazel.

"Well?" she said. "What did Monsieur Gentil want?"

"He just wanted to tell us that Frankie called and she made it to Istanbul," Ned began. "She hasn't seen Dad yet, but she wanted to know how we were. So Monsieur Gentil told her we'd made it safely here and he'd talked to us. She wanted to know if you'd looked at the painting yet. . . ."

"Why?" Hazel asked. "Did she say something about Paolo Cafazzo?"

Ned shook his head.

"No, but it sounds like maybe you were right before, Hazel," he replied. "Frankie told Monsieur Gentil she hoped it wasn't too big a shock for you, finally having a portrait of our mother."

"Our *mother*?" Hazel repeated. "But . . . that means . . ."

"I know." Ned nodded. "You've definitely got the wrong painting."

Hazel's eyes widened. "Frankie said Dad had some paintings with him when he left. And she said he was in a hurry. What if he switched paintings by mistake? What if Dad took the wrong painting to Istanbul?"

Ned scratched his head. "Maybe that's why he's in jail."

10

The cousins were determined to show Ville St-Pierre to Hazel and Ned. Her mind still reeling from Monsieur Gentil's phone call, Hazel went along, but she could scarcely take in the scattering of quaint shops or the brightly painted boats in the harbor.

They had just sat down on the steps of the empty band shell to eat ice-cream cones when Charlotte pulled up in her truck.

"Hi, Frumps," she called. "Getting to know each other? Listen, I'm sorry to bother you, but I need a hand. A couple of horses up at the Deacons' farm were hurt when a stray dog got into their paddock. It doesn't sound too serious, but I could use some help corraling them and calming them down so I can inspect the damage. Any volunteers?"

Matt, Mark, and Deirdre were already tossing their cones into the garbage bin.

"What about you guys?" Mark said over his shoulder as he climbed into the front seat. "Hazel? Oliver? Ned?"

"No, thanks," Oliver answered. "I got my foot trampled last time I helped—remember?"

Ned looked at Hazel; she shook her head. Last year she had been thrown by a cranky mare during riding lessons at boarding school and had landed in a pile of manure. Hazel wasn't crazy about horses.

"No, thanks," Ned replied. "If you've got enough to manage without us, I think we'll just walk home."

With Mark's long, skinny arm waving out the rear window of the cab, the truck disappeared down the darkening street.

"So, Oliver, your foot got trampled by a horse?" Ned asked as they began retracing their steps toward home.

"What?" said Oliver. "Oh, that. No, it wasn't the horse. We were helping Charlotte with a sick foal, and Mark tripped over a barn cat. He landed on my big toe. Mark, I mean, not the cat. It really hurt."

The route back to Land's End Lane took them past a basketball court. Dusk had fallen while they were finishing their ice cream, and it was getting hard to see. But as they approached the court, Hazel could hear voices: a low whine, a higher-pitched giggle, and a quiet, bored tone.

As the three Frump children drew alongside the court, the ballplayers turned to stare at them. Hazel recognized the two fair-haired boys who had soaped cars on the ferry and the dark-haired one named Hank.

Beside her, Ned sucked in his breath, while Oliver made a tiny, uncomfortable sound. They'd recognized the boys too. Hazel wished the ballplayers weren't within earshot, so she could ask Oliver who they were and whether they meant trouble. She wondered what their connection was to Clive Pritchard.

But the three boys had stopped talking now and were simply watching the Frumps. Hazel nodded curtly toward them, then turned to Oliver and said, "We should be getting home. Let's go."

Oliver looked relieved, but they had taken only a few steps when the smaller boy called out, "Hey, Chump! Olly Chump! Where are you going?"

Oliver looked at Hazel. He whispered so that only she and Ned could hear, "He calls me that to hurt my feelings. Just ignore it."

"Hey, Chump! Who're your friends?" It was the whiny boy, trying to sound threatening. In the dark, deserted park it should have worked. But when Hazel glanced at him, she remembered how this boy had cowered before the ferryman.

"You know, maybe ignoring these guys isn't working out so well for you," Ned muttered.

"Let's just go." Oliver tugged at Hazel's sleeve.

Thwack! A basketball, thrown hard, landed squarely between Oliver's shoulder blades, sending him sprawling onto the ground. As Hazel and Ned helped him to his feet, Oliver gulped to keep from crying.

"I'm okay," Oliver said shakily. "Let's just get out of here."

Hazel picked up the basketball and turned to face the boys. "That was clever," she said flatly, her voice calm. "Not to mention brave, whipping a ball at somebody's back . . . somebody smaller than you."

She made no move to return the ball. Instead, Hazel began bouncing it up and down on the path beside her—a slow, steady dribble she maintained without ever glancing down at the ball, not even when she switched from one hand to the other. She kept her gaze on the three boys. Waiting.

The one called Hank, who had looked so bored on the ferry, didn't look bored now. He'd been staring at Hazel. Now he turned and cuffed the youngest boy on the head.

"What did you do that for?" Hank asked. "Apologize to . . . Oliver."

"No way," came the unrepentant reply as the

youngest boy rubbed his head. "What's your problem, Hank?"

"*My* problem?" repeated Hank in disbelief. "I don't have a problem. But I'm starting to think maybe you do."

The whiny boy stuck out his lip. "You *guyyyyyys,* make her give me my ball back."

Hazel laughed. She was dribbling the ball faster now, passing it behind her back and between her legs, still never taking her eyes off them.

"Make me," she taunted. "You want the ball back, how about you *play* me?"

"Play you?" repeated the middle boy stupidly. "You mean, for the ball? You mean the winner keeps *my* ball?"

"Yeah, Einstein," answered Hazel.

"But . . . but that's not fair. It's *my* ball," the boy asserted.

Hank looked like he was trying not to smile. "Look, say you're sorry, Kenny, and maybe she'll give back Billy's ball."

"Or maybe you guys don't know how to play?" Hazel continued. "Maybe you just stand around *holding* the ball 'cause you think it makes you look cool."

Hazel was spinning the ball now, balancing it atop one finger. She and Alysha had spent months practicing that particular trick last year. Billy—that appeared to be the name of the whiny boy—let his jaw hang slack.

"Hey, Ned, maybe that boy didn't mean to hit Oliver in the back," Hazel suggested conversationally. "Maybe that was his idea of a pass."

"This is crazy." Hank shook his head.

"Um, Hazel?" whispered Oliver. "You could just give them their ball back. I'm okay, really."

Hazel smiled reassuringly at Oliver, then shook her head. Even Kenny was wide-eyed as she rolled the ball across her shoulders and down her arm, catching it in her right hand. She strolled toward the asphalt court, dribbling the ball.

"Hey there . . . Kenny, is that your name?" she said. "My cousin Oliver says to ignore you. But I think we're all done ignoring you. I think it's time to pay attention—what do you say? Let's all pay really close attention to how well Kenny can play ball."

"You're weird." Kenny scowled.

"You have no idea," sighed Ned. He had followed Hazel onto the court.

"Three on three," Hazel announced briskly. "You three: Kenny, Hank, and Billy? Are those your names? It's you three against Oliver, me, and my brother. Each bucket is one point. First team to fifteen points wins."

"Uh, Hazel, I don't really play basketball that much." Oliver sounded embarrassed.

"You'll be fine," Hazel assured him quietly. "Just keep moving."

It was the shortest game Hazel had ever played. Hank turned out to be the best player of the three, but that wasn't saying much. Besides, when Oliver dropped the ball and Hank scooped it up to score on an easy layup, Hazel could tell his heart wasn't in it. Kenny and Billy wanted to win, but it was plain to everyone that simply wasn't going to happen.

None of the three boys seemed to have a clue about how to play defense, and Hazel drained jump shot after jump shot without so much as a hand in her face. After she had run up nine points, including a shot from the far end of the court, Hazel figured it was time to set up her teammates. She knew Ned liked to shoot from the corner. Stripping the ball from Kenny's hands, she fed it to her brother. Ned drained two baskets in a row from the corner. His third attempt clanged off the rim, but before Billy could take a single step, Hazel had grabbed the rebound.

Oliver's contributions consisted mostly of jumping up and down excitedly and clapping every time Hazel scored, but she was determined to make her little cousin part of the victory. After another easy basket, Hazel called a time-out. Walking over to Oliver, she whispered, "When you hear me count to three, I want you to throw the ball up at the basket, hard as you can."

Her cousin gaped at her.

"I can't . . . I can't shoot," he croaked.

"Trust me," Hazel said as she walked away. "Okay, game on!" she hollered.

Oliver stood his ground at the foul line. Glancing nervously at the approaching Kenny, he bounced the ball once, twice . . .

Hazel broke into a run; as she neared the basket, she yelled, "Onetwothree!"

She turned her head in time to see Oliver hurl the ball skyward just as Kenny and Billy converged on him. If she had the timing right—Hazel leaped, twisted, and caught the ball in midair and lofted it into the basket.

"Hey, Billy! I thought you were guarding her," Kenny called. "Nice job!"

"It's not my fault," Billy said.

Hank laughed. "Nice alley-oop," he told Hazel.

Kenny scowled. He didn't like losing. Now, doesn't that just figure, Hazel told herself as she drove past Hank to the basket. On top of everything else, he's a sore loser.

Crunch! Hazel's ribs were squeezed as Billy and Kenny slammed into her from opposite sides. She fell to the ground, Billy landing heavily on top of her. Above their heads, the basketball she'd just tossed up rolled twice around the rim before dropping through the hoop into Hank's waiting hands. He glanced back at Hazel in time to see Kenny, who'd kept his balance, grind his foot into Hazel's wrist as she struggled to get to her feet.

"Hey!" cried Hank as Hazel gasped in pain.

Without stopping to acknowledge what he'd done, Kenny darted forward, grabbing the ball from Hank's hands, to shoot from just below the basket. The ball bounced off the backboard and Kenny caught it again, taking another shot. He didn't seem to notice that all the other players had stopped, or that Hazel and Billy were still on the ground.

"I scored! Did you see that?" Kenny crowed as, on his third try, the ball rolled through the hoop.

"Yeah, that was great, Pritchard," said Hank sarcastically. He helped Hazel stand up.

She stared at Hank. *What* had he called Kenny?

"Are you okay?" Hank asked her. "We should probably take you to a doctor or something."

No one made a move to help Billy. He flapped one arm feebly to draw attention and began to moan piteously.

"Ow, ow, somebody help me up! I think my leg is busted. I think I broke my ribs."

Oliver and Ned each raised a single eyebrow; then Oliver extended a hand to the middle boy, who staggered upright. Ignoring his friend, Hank asked Hazel again whether she was all right. She nodded. Actually, her wrist was probably sprained, and the truth was it hurt like heck. But Hazel wasn't going to give these boys the satisfaction of knowing that.

"Hey, where's your defense now?" taunted Kenny, who had managed to sink another basket, this time on his fourth try. The ball rolled toward Ned, who picked it up soberly.

"The game's over, Pritchard. They won," said Hank irritably. "Stop being such a jerk."

"They didn't win," Kenny answered back. "She said first team to get fifteen! That means they still need one more basket!"

"Don't be stupid," Hank said.

Pritchard. He really *had* said Pritchard. Kenny Pritchard. For a moment Hazel couldn't move. Then she shook her head. It was a coincidence, it just *had* to be.

But if it wasn't, well, it was too late now.

Hazel didn't even look at Kenny. She lifted her head and stared at the basket. Wordlessly, she held out her good arm toward Ned. He tossed the ball gently to her.

"Now *you're* being ridiculous," muttered Hank, gazing at her in disbelief.

Hazel hoisted the ball to her shoulder. It was no longer dusk; night had fallen and the net was barely visible. She narrowed her eyes. Then she lofted the ball, using only one arm, high into the air.

Six pairs of eyes followed its graceful arc until silently, neatly, the ball dropped precisely through the hoop and came to rest on the asphalt below.

There was a moment of silence. Then several voices spoke at once.

"I can't believe you," Hank said flatly.

"My leg hurts," whimpered Billy.

"What happens to the ball?" demanded Kenny.

Hazel looked wearily at Oliver.

"Keep it," Oliver said to Billy.

"Yeah, you guys could use the practice," Ned added.

Hazel turned and led the Frumps out of the park.

"Wait up," Hank cried.

But the cousins kept walking. Hazel gazed at the lighted homes, wondering if one of them was Kenny Pritchard's. He probably was related to Clive, but how? Was Clive his father? Did he know how messed up Kenny was? Kenny could have broken her wrist, and she was pretty sure he wouldn't have cared.

In silence, they walked past the closed shops toward Land's End Lane. As they passed a dimly lit storefront selling art and antiques, Ned stopped abruptly. He stared at a small oil painting at the back of the window.

"What now?" Hazel asked.

"Hazel, does that painting remind you of anything?" Ned asked, his voice barely concealing his excitement.

Hazel sighed. Her wrist was really quite sore, and she was tired. She just wanted to get to Land's End. She peered through the glass.

The painting did look familiar. It was in the same dark, Romantic style as the Paolo Cafazzo painting of the castle she'd carefully hidden in her room earlier that day. The setting for this painting was also a storm at night, and in the foreground the painter had placed a violent shipwreck; in the background there was an island with a ruined old tower, crumbling into the sea.

"Hey, that reminds me of our tower," Oliver said. "What do you think, Ned?"

A shiver ran down Hazel's spine. It *did* look like the Martello tower where she had spotted Richard C. Plevit that morning.

"Yeah, kinda," Ned replied, his voice deliberately casual. "It also reminds me a lot of this painting I saw once on the internet."

He turned to look meaningfully at Hazel, as if to make sure she understood him: another work by the supposedly obscure Paolo Cafazzo. She nodded once, not wishing to attract Oliver's attention. But he seemed to have something else on his mind.

"Hey, Hazel," Oliver said, scuffing the ground with the toe of his sneaker. "I'm really sorry about tonight—about getting your hand hurt and all."

Hazel shook her head at him and smiled. "Don't be silly. You weren't the one who stomped on my wrist," she said. "Besides, I'm the oldest and I was the one who wouldn't walk away. But you know what? I'm not sorry at all."

Oliver smiled at her, relief showing in his eyes.

"We should probably get going," said Ned, pulling his gaze away from the shop window. "Maybe tomorrow we could come back and take a closer look, when this place is open."

"That one's really just for tourists," Oliver said as they trudged down the road. "Nobody around here much likes the guy who owns it."

"Why?" asked Ned.

"Well, you know that boy Kenny—the one who hurt Hazel?" Oliver asked. "It's his uncle Clive who owns the store. Nobody likes Clive. He hasn't really lived on the island for years, but he comes back now and then to visit Kenny's parents."

Ned appeared to trip over nothing, stumbling but not quite falling. Oliver put out a hand to steady him.

"You okay?" Oliver asked.

"It's too soon to tell," Ned muttered.

Hazel could feel the dusty stone floor beneath her cheek. She could see the night sky through the tall, arched window. Her legs felt like lead; they refused to move.

She couldn't be back here, not again.

She tried to move her arms. A stab of pain shot through her hand.

"Why am I here?" Hazel pleaded. "I don't understand."

There was no answer.

The stars cast a cold, bright light over the tower room. Hazel could tell now that many of the shapes covered by white sheets were artists' easels.

The brightest beam of moonlight fell across the easel directly in front of her, causing its canvas shroud to glow. Suddenly, Hazel knew what to do. She had to reveal what was hidden underneath.

Hazel struggled to get up. She had to find out—everyone was counting on her. But there was so little time. And she couldn't move.

"I'll never do it," Hazel sobbed. "It's too hard. It's not fair. I can't, I can't."

Yes, you can. You will.

The woman sounded so sure, so calm, that for a moment Hazel believed her. But then came a man's bitter laugh. She'd never met him, but Hazel knew at once who it was—and the sound froze her blood.

"No, you won't," said Clive Pritchard.

Hazel awoke as suddenly as if she had been thrown from a horse, feeling bruised and sore. She was drenched in sweat, and the sound of her breathing filled the small circular room. Eyes wide, she scanned her surroundings. She was in the guest room above Deirdre's room, in one of the towers at Land's End. She was *not* trapped. She could move her arms and legs, although her wrist, where Kenny Pritchard had tromped on it the night before, was swollen and aching. Early-morning light was filling the perfectly round room.

She was alone.

The sun was just rising, and the sky was dark and streaked with pink-and-gray clouds. Hazel knew she wouldn't be able to return to sleep; the dream had been too disturbing. Besides, the pain in her wrist was intense. Opening the tall curved window beside her bed, Hazel felt a gust of cooling wind on her face. The trees in the orchard were rustling, and the lake beyond looked black, swollen, and menacing.

If sleep wasn't possible, breakfast was, Hazel decided. She checked first to make sure the Paolo Cafazzo painting was still wrapped in a sweatshirt and tucked into a secret compartment under the window seat.

Then Hazel made her way carefully down the stairs and into the deserted kitchen. It didn't surprise her that the others had slept in. They had all stayed up late last night, rehashing the game and hearing about the injured horses.

Hazel scooped a handful of ice cubes from the freezer, wrapped them awkwardly in a dish towel, and held the makeshift ice bag over her wrist. It took time to fill a tray with cereal and orange juice using only her right hand, but once she had the tray carefully braced between hip and arm, Hazel was able to unlatch the screen door and maneuver her way onto the porch.

"Good morning," Mark said cheerfully. He was stretched out on a wicker sofa that was not quite long enough to accommodate him.

Hazel jumped and almost dropped the tray.

"I didn't know anybody else was up," she said.

"Just us," Mark answered. "I think it's going to storm. I heard a noise, so I got up to check it out. It was just the shed door blowing open. But I latched it last night, so that means we're talking about a pretty strong wind. Rain can't be far behind. I thought I'd just lie here and watch the storm build. Don't you love storms?"

"I guess," Hazel answered dubiously.

She lifted the bowl of cereal from the tray and winced, realizing it would hurt too much to try to hold it in her left hand while eating with her right. Mark sized up the situation instantly. Unfolding himself from the sofa, he pulled a chair over to the table and pushed Hazel down into it. Then he gently lifted her left arm, supporting the bruised wrist with one hand. Despite his care, Hazel flinched.

"I think Kenny Pritchard did more damage than you thought," her cousin remarked.

Hazel reached for the ice and covered her wrist with it.

"I've been injured before. It hurts, but it's just a sprain," she assured him.

"Can you move your fingers?" Mark asked.

Hazel waggled them obligingly.

"Hmm. I think that means it can't be broken, but Matt's the one who wants to be a doctor. Or a vet.

Anyway, drink your juice," he said. "I'll be right back."

Hazel expected the screen door to close behind him, but the breeze caught it and pinned it open against the outside wall. She could hear the wind gathering force; tree boughs were creaking, leaves were fluttering. Out on the lawn, a flowerpot toppled over.

"Wow, the rain can't be far off now," Mark said, returning. He had to raise his voice to be heard over the din. "I called Charlotte; she's having car trouble, so I'm going to go pick her up in a few minutes. You wanna wait out here, or inside where it's quieter?"

"Why are you getting Charlotte?"

"Well, she lent the truck to a friend and her van is in the shop."

"I get the car-trouble thing, but I meant why is she coming over?" Hazel asked.

"Doc McCormack is on vacation, and somebody should look at your wrist," Mark explained. "Charlotte said it doesn't sound like it's broken, but she wants to check it out anyway."

Hazel nodded. There was a flash of lightning, followed almost instantly by a deafening clap of thunder. Mark and Hazel both jumped.

"Look, I'd better get Charly before the storm really hits," Mark said. "You go inside, okay?"

Hazel nodded. But she stayed on the porch, watching, as Mark dashed to the truck. The pickup hadn't been gone more than a minute before the rain started. It was heavier than any rain she had ever seen. In a few minutes she could no longer make out the lake, or the orchard beyond the first row of trees. She stood up and took a step toward the door; the roof above the porch began to clatter, as if a giant was tossing marbles down onto it.

"Whoa! That's serious hail!"

Matt was standing just inside the kitchen, his face pressed against the screen. Hazel turned to see small white pellets hitting the lawn. The willow trees that marked the way to the pebbly beach bent beneath the force of the wind. Hazel wondered if they would break. The sound of the hail on the roof was so loud, she didn't notice Matt had joined her on the porch until he was shouting in her ear. "The wind's coming from two directions!"

She looked back at him blankly. Who cared where the wind was coming from? But Matt yanked her into the kitchen, pulling the door closed behind them. Inside, it was quieter, although Hazel could hear voices and footsteps on the stairs. It sounded like someone running.

"Listen, city slicker, when you have hail and wind coming from two directions, you sometimes get tornados," Matt explained, grabbing a flashlight from the cupboard.

"Wow," Hazel breathed, glancing back toward the door. "So, do we go to the cellar?"

Matt nodded his answer just as Oliver and Ned barreled around the corner. Both boys were slightly out of breath, and behind their glasses, their eyes were wide with excitement. Ned had borrowed Oliver's clothes, and as Hazel looked at them, clad in matching sweatpants and T-shirts emblazoned with the stenciled image of Albert Einstein, she reflected again that the pair could be twins, they looked so much alike.

A yawning Deirdre was bringing up the rear, dressed in the faded tank top and gym shorts she had slept in, with pillow marks still creasing the skin on her cheek.

"We found Deirdre, but we couldn't find Mark," Oliver said, his voice squeaking with excitement.

"He went to get Charlotte," Hazel said. She held out her wrist. "He thought she should make sure Kenny didn't break anything."

Matt opened a door, and all five of them piled down a steep staircase into the cellar below. It wasn't at all what Hazel had expected.

"This is very cool," observed Ned, looking around. "Not your ordinary, everyday dungeon!"

The castle had been built in the late 1800s, Deirdre had told Hazel, but the cellar looked as if it might be even older. The walls were made of stone, and the timbers above their heads had been hewn from giant trees. The air was cool, much cooler than upstairs, and somebody had seen fit to stock the cellar with brass lamps and old armchairs, faded cushions, a sofa, and some trunks and packing crates.

"We used to play down here when we were little," Deirdre explained. "We'd build forts and clubhouses and make a lot of noise. I bet inside that case there's still . . . aha!"

From the largest trunk she pulled a stack of comic books and held them aloft.

"Behold our reading entertainment while we wait for the all clear," Oliver told Ned. The two boys tore into the pile.

"Meanwhile, how long ago did Mark leave to get Charlotte?" Matt asked Hazel. He had lowered his voice so that the boys couldn't hear, and Hazel could tell he was worried.

"I sort of lost track of time, watching the storm," she confessed. "But I know it started to rain after the truck left the driveway."

Matthew's face relaxed and he let out his breath. "That's all right then," he said. "Charlotte's only a couple of miles away. He'll have had enough time to make it to her place and take shelter in her cellar."

Hazel was relieved. She wouldn't have wanted Mark to be caught out in the storm because of her.

Deirdre and Matt proposed giving Hazel a tour of

the cellars. As Deirdre chattered about how there hadn't been a tornado in the area for ages, Matt led the way through a warren of rooms, some empty and cavernous, some cozy and furnished. Deirdre pointed out the wine cellar, stacked with racks and racks of dusty bottles, and a room filled entirely with miniature trains and endless looping tracks.

Once Matt had demonstrated just how the electric trains worked, making them loop around the room a few times, the older Frumps all agreed it was time to see whether the storm was still raging. Ned and Oliver were still engrossed in the early adventures of Superman and had no interest in going back upstairs, so Matt, Deirdre, and Hazel headed to the kitchen.

"It sounds like the storm's passed," Matt said as they crossed the floor. Opening the screen door, he let out a low whistle.

"It did a lot of damage," Hazel said.

"Let's go up to the lookout tower and get a better view," Deirdre suggested. "Maybe it really *was* a tornado."

The tower's worn flagstones were slick with rain, and Hazel felt even less safe than she had during her previous visit to the lookout. Still, it did provide a dramatic view of the damage the storm had caused. Several of the apple trees had lost limbs, and one of the old willows, completely uprooted, lay by the shore of the lake. The wind had picked up two large garden urns and set them down, unharmed and right end up, about fifty feet away from their original positions on the lawn, and had also flattened the garden shed.

Deirdre pointed to the driveway.

"Looks like we have a visitor."

A black pickup had pulled up in front of Land's End, and a slender man in jeans and a cap emerged.

"He's going to the front door, but the boys won't hear. They're still in the basement," said Deirdre.

The man, having had no answer at the front door, was walking around the side of the castle, as if looking for another way in. A gust of wind blew his cap into the air. He caught it quickly, but not before the three of them had seen his face.

"Isn't that Kenny Pritchard's uncle?" asked Matt, just as Deirdre yelled, "Yoohoo! Mr. Pritchard!"

Clive Pritchard glanced around.

"No! Get back," Hazel hissed, stumbling toward the trapdoor. In her haste she staggered against Matt, and the two fell heavily to the floor. As Deirdre bent to help them up, Hazel pulled her down on top of them.

Matt looked at Hazel. "Clive's got a reputation around here, and it's not great. So I know why *I* don't feel like inviting him in . . . but what's your story?"

"Well, I don't want to be melodramatic or anything," Hazel said with an unconvincing laugh.

"If you ask me, I think you're there already," Deirdre said, rubbing her arm.

"Well . . . we saw Clive Pritchard in the city, before we left," Hazel began. "He and this friend of his were arguing with my neighbor. And then Ned and I saw him on the ferry, and then I think I saw his friend after we arrived. Remember, Deirdre, the man in the Martello tower?"

Deirdre shook her head, then stopped abruptly. "Oh, yeah. Hazel said she saw someone, but when I looked, I didn't see anyone there," she told Matt.

"Anyway, the thing is, he's part of the reason we left the city," Hazel admitted. "Our apartment was burgled, and we think he had something to do with it. There's more stuff that has to do with my dad, and Ned and I were going to tell you guys all about it today. Just trust me: I don't think we want to let him in."

Matt was already moving toward the trapdoor.

"Where are you going?" asked Hazel.

"This isn't the city, Hazel," Matt replied. "We don't lock our doors around here. Not in the daytime."

"Oh, no," Hazel cried. "The boys are downstairs—alone!"

But Matt had already vanished down the circular staircase.

12

Hazel flung herself down the stairs after her cousin. The staircase was completely enclosed, but at each floor there was a door leading to a passageway beyond. When Hazel reached the first door, it was ajar, and she could see Matt in the hall. He was standing beside a small wooden table, holding an old-fashioned telephone receiver in his hand. He turned to face Hazel as she entered, a breathless Deirdre at her heels.

"Matt—what's going on? What's wrong?" Deirdre asked.

"The phone line's dead."

Hazel stared at Matt.

"What about a cell phone?" Hazel asked.

Matt shook his head. "They don't work at Land's End."

Hazel bit her lip. They were completely cut off from the village, or from any outside help. As she watched Deirdre fumble with the phone, Hazel's mind began to race. Why was the phone dead? Was it the storm? Or had someone cut the line?

"I think we should go find the boys," Deirdre said, setting down the phone. "I still think you guys are crazy, and I'm sure Mr. Pritchard doesn't mean any harm, but . . . well, we might as well all stick together."

"What if he's already in the house?" Hazel asked. "Can we get to the boys without running into him?"

Matt's eyes reflected Hazel's concern. "C'mon, you two—the secret staircase!"

"Secret staircase?" Hazel asked. But Matt and Deirdre were already pelting down the corridor.

Later, when Hazel tried to reconstruct their flight in her mind, she found she could recall nothing but a blur of hallways and rooms, some of which she knew Deirdre had shown her before. There were occasional pauses, when Matt would stop dead in his tracks, put his fingers to his lips, and listen. They would hear footsteps, and then Matt would change direction, leading the girls away from the sound, down new corridors and through different rooms, but somehow always working their way toward the secret staircase.

The footsteps had to belong to Clive Pritchard, Hazel figured. Deirdre suggested he was just there to offer help after the storm. But if that was the case, Hazel would have expected him to call their names. At the very least, he should have been calling, "Hello? Anybody home?" Instead, it seemed the man was making as little noise as possible.

They had arrived in what appeared to be a music room; a baby grand piano stood in one corner, an old harp next to it. But there was no time to look around, because Matt was tapping one of the wooden wall panels and it was sliding back, opening onto a dank, dusty set of steps.

"Come on," Deirdre said impatiently as she pushed Hazel in front of her. Matt had already headed down the stairs without looking back to see if they were following.

"I can't see," Hazel whispered.

"Me neither, but our eyes will adjust," said Deirdre. "If you let me squeeze past, I'll go first, and you can hold on to me as we go."

It was a tight fit, but they managed it somehow. Hazel heard the panel slide closed behind her, and then she was shuffling down the dark steps, her right hand clamped firmly on Deirdre's shoulder, her injured left tentatively brushing against the wall. It seemed to take forever to reach the bottom. Matt was waiting in a small room filled with boxes. At least, in the gloom Hazel thought she could make out large, cratelike objects here and there.

"I can hear Ned and Oliver," Hazel whispered excitedly.

"Yes, and I *don't* hear that Pritchard guy," Matt said. "I'll grab the boys. You girls stay here. And keep quiet!"

As they waited for him to return, Deirdre passed the time wondering in whispers whether Clive Pritchard would suddenly jump out of the shadows behind her, or whether he was lying in wait in the next room, ready to pounce on Matt and the boys. Hazel passed the time wondering whether the feeling of crawling skin on her neck was nerves, dust, or a tarantula out for a stroll. As their eyes adjusted, Deirdre pointed out a cigarette butt on the floor near their feet, and then a lighter on a nearby steamer trunk.

"I guess someone's been experimenting with smoking!" she said. "Wait until I tell Dad."

"Who knows how long it's been there?" Hazel whispered. "Maybe it was Uncle Seamus who was doing the experimenting, or my dad."

"Hey. What's up?"

It was Ned's voice, and he was shining a bright light in their eyes.

"Quit that!" Deirdre scolded, her voice a little too loud. Ned pointed the flashlight at their feet.

"I thought I told you to be quiet," Matt said from

the darkness as he claimed the flashlight.

"What's going on?" asked Oliver. "If this is some sort of kooky game, can we play it later? 'Cause Ned and me were having a perfectly good time on our own."

"Ned and *I*," corrected Deirdre automatically.

"No. Me. You weren't playing. You guys took off ages ago," Oliver answered.

"Enough," Matt said. "Listen!"

Everyone looked at Matt expectantly.

"Well?" Deirdre asked. "We're listening. What?"

"No, *listen*," Matt said through gritted teeth. "Do you hear anything? Or anyone?"

It was so still, all Hazel could hear was Oliver's slightly adenoidal breathing. Then—

"Footsteps," said Ned. "Is Mark back with Charlotte?"

The footsteps were getting closer and louder.

"That's too heavy to be Mark or Charlotte," Deirdre whispered.

"Besides, they'd be calling out to us," Matt muttered. "We need to get out of here. Follow me."

He led them deeper into the box room. The beam of the flashlight illuminated the stacks of packing crates and revealed the existence of a low door behind the staircase. Matt opened it and gestured to the others to follow.

"I'll go first with the light, then Oliver and Ned,"

he said in a whisper so quiet it was barely audible. "Then Hazel, then Deirdre—and Deirdre, you have to shut the door. Okay? Everybody keep close together."

Nobody said a word until they were all inside the passageway with the door closed behind them. Hazel tried not to think about how much darker and dirtier and insect friendly this passage looked than anywhere else she'd ventured that day. She had the oddest sensation that there was something familiar about this place. A shiver ran through her body.

"Kind of cold in here, isn't it?" Deirdre whispered, giving her arm a sympathetic squeeze. "I wish we'd had time to get dressed; these pajamas aren't very warm."

"Um, can I ask a question?" It was Ned, sounding determined to remain calm.

"Shoot," Matt answered as he began leading the way down the corridor.

"Who are we running from?"

Hazel put her hand on her brother's arm. "It's Pritchard," she whispered.

"Kenny?" squeaked Oliver, sounding alarmed.

"His uncle," said Matt.

"Can I ask another question?"

"You just did," Matt said.

"Where are we running *to*?"

There was silence for a moment. Hazel began to

wonder if Matt knew the answer.

"Of course, we're not actually *running*," Deirdre said.

Matt ignored his sister; when he spoke it was to answer Ned.

"Dad always said there were secret passages leading out of the castle," he told Ned. "He showed me the entrance to this one once and promised me we'd explore it someday. The guy who built this place supposedly thought secret passages would make it more romantic. But there were rumors about smugglers using them too."

"Dad never told *me* any of this," said Deirdre, wounded.

"Well, he didn't want any of us getting lost down here," Matt said. "He wasn't sure how structurally sound it was. He was worried there might be cave-ins."

"Hey, now, *there's* a happy thought." Hazel was trying to sound casual, but there was a slight tremble to her voice. She couldn't shake the feeling that she had been here before. But that was impossible. Wasn't it? She felt Ned pat her arm.

"Well, I'm sure we don't have to go very far into this passage," Matt said. "I just want to make sure we're not being followed."

They shuffled along in silence for a few more minutes before anyone spoke again.

"Did you hear that?" Ned said suddenly.

"What?" Matt asked.

"I heard a door opening," Ned replied.

"Run!" said Matt, following his own order instantly.

It was amazing how quickly and quietly they were all able to move, despite the narrowness of the passage and the roughness of the ground. Ned stumbled once, but Hazel grabbed her brother before he could fall. Without thinking, she used her injured hand, forgetting it was hurt until the pain sliced through her wrist. She bit back tears; Ned paused, realizing something was wrong.

"I'm okay." Hazel gave Ned's shoulder a gentle shove with her good arm. "Just keep going."

A few seconds later, all slightly out of breath, the cousins found themselves at a place where the passage widened into what was almost a small room. Here the tunnel branched off in several directions, and Matt appeared to be trying to decide which passage to take. Hazel was sure they should go right. It was like the day in science class when they'd held the magnet in one hand and the paper clip in the other. She could feel a pull. She opened her mouth to say, "Let's go right," but was distracted by faint sounds from behind them in the passageway.

"Left," Matt whispered, and they all obeyed.

Presently, Hazel realized the tunnel was growing lighter, and she could see her brother and Oliver much more distinctly.

"We're coming to the end," Matt announced with satisfaction. "There's an opening just ahead."

A minute later they were stumbling out of the low mouth of a cave. Blinking in the light, Hazel saw that they had arrived at a beach. But it wasn't the pebbly beach near the house, and it wasn't Sandy Bay, where they had picnicked and swum what seemed like a lifetime ago.

"Where the heck are we?" Ned asked. He'd taken off his spectacles and was busily polishing them. But a quick glance told Hazel he wasn't worried—just covered in dirt and dust from the passageway.

"This is the cove just beyond Sandy Bay," Deirdre said in wonder. "I never knew there was a cave here."

They stood for a few minutes staring at each other. Nobody seemed quite sure what to do next. Matt spoke first.

"I'll sneak back into the tunnel a ways and see if Clive is still following," he said slowly. "You guys wait here. If you hear me give the signal, start running."

"What's the signal?" asked Ned.

"How about I just holler, 'Look out!' or 'He's coming!'?" Matt said wearily as he reentered the cave.

Hazel plunked herself down on the shale beach and

rested her head on her knees. At least it isn't raining, she thought as she gazed at the clear sky. The lake looked calm; the water lapped the rocks along the shore with a soothing rhythm.

Hazel closed her eyes. She didn't think she'd have the energy to run if Clive Pritchard himself walked out of the cave.

"Pritchard must have turned the other way at that fork in the passage," Matt announced as he emerged from the cave once more. "Either that or he went back to the house. There's no sign of him, anyway."

"So what do we do now?" asked Oliver.

"Mark and Charlotte are bound to make it home soon; we'll rest for a bit, then walk back to the house."

They sat in silence for a few minutes, listening to the gulls keening overhead. The sun was struggling through the clouds now, and the warmth felt good on Hazel's skin. She examined her cousin. His face was grimy and set in lines of worry.

"Thanks for getting us out of there," Hazel told Matt.

Her cousin shrugged. "I just wish I knew where that guy went," he said. "Not to mention what he wanted."

Hazel looked at her feet. She hated the thought that she and Ned might have brought danger to Land's End.

"At first I figured he'd come here to complain about your basketball game with Kenny," Matt continued. "But when you said your place had been burgled, and then the phone was dead . . ."

"Mr. Pritchard was sneaking around, not stomping around," Deirdre said. "So was he really chasing us? Or was he snooping?"

After a pause, Ned asked, "Is anybody else hungry?" And suddenly five stomachs were acutely aware of the passage of time.

"I am," Matt said. "If everybody's had a chance to catch their breath, I say we head home."

By tacit agreement, they walked back along the rocky shoreline instead of reentering the tunnel. At Sandy Bay, the children could see more of the damage the storm had wrought. The white dunes were littered with driftwood and bits of plastic and other debris that had washed ashore.

As the bedraggled troupe made their way out of the orchard, clambering through wet grass and over fallen tree limbs, they heard Mark and Charlotte calling their names.

"Over here!" called Deirdre, and in minutes they were all together on the side lawn.

"We were getting worried about you," Charlotte said. "It took us forever to get here. The roads were blocked."

"We tried to call, but all the lines were down," Mark said.

So Clive Pritchard hadn't cut the phone lines to the castle. Hazel felt a little foolish. But then she thought about the newspaper clipping with the picture of her father in handcuffs and the photo of his "partner" Clive Pritchard. The foolish feeling evaporated.

"We tried to call you guys too," Matt said. "We wanted to make sure you were okay."

"Well, we spent some time in Charly's cellar, and let me tell you, that's not a place you want to linger," Mark said. "I vote we take up a collection and buy this nice woman a chair for her basement . . . maybe a lightbulb, too. Anyway, we survived. Where were you guys, though?"

"And why are you all still in your pajamas?" Charlotte asked, cocking her head to one side.

"It's a long story," Matt said. "Breakfast first."

"First things first," Charlotte said as they gathered in the kitchen. "I need to take a look at Hazel's wrist."

After a few minutes of careful prodding, Charlotte pronounced herself satisfied that the wrist was not broken.

"But I do think it's a nasty sprain." Charlotte frowned. "We should probably go into Frontenac to have it looked at by a doctor."

"Right *now*?" Hazel groaned. She was tired and hungry. A bath or shower also might be nice; in that tunnel, who knew what sorts of insects might have decided to hitch a ride in her hair.

Charlotte laughed. "Actually, no," she answered. "Right *now* I'm putting your arm in a sling to support your wrist. Right *now* I'm giving you these pills to help with the pain and swelling—and they're people pills, nothing for dogs or sheep or anything like that, so don't give me that look. And right *now* we're all going to get something to eat. Then one of you is going to please make me some coffee while somebody—anybody—fills me in on what's been going on here."

The cousins were obviously used to Charlotte ordering them about. Within a few minutes Hazel's arm was resting in a sling, Matt had set the table, bacon was frying on the stove, seven glasses had been filled with orange juice, coffee was percolating, and fruit, bread, and cheese had been slapped onto plates. Ned and Oliver were explaining how Hazel had come by her injury in the first place.

"Oliver," Charlotte said, when the full story of the basketball game had been recounted, "why on earth didn't you tell any of us this child was bullying you?"

Oliver squirmed. "It's embarrassing," he finally managed to say.

"Plus, his teacher said if he ignored it, Kenny would leave him alone," Ned said.

"I always said that teacher was a fool," Mark said.

Matt put his hand on Oliver's shoulder. "Hey, Squirt, bullying is never the fault of the person being bullied."

"Right," agreed Charlotte. "Also, it's not something that's easy to fix on your own. We'll get this sorted out together, all right?"

Oliver was studying his shoes, but he nodded silently.

Matt gave Deirdre and Hazel a meaningful look and pushed his chair back from the table. Squaring his broad shoulders and leaning forward slightly in his chair, he took a deep breath and began. "Hey, uh, Charly? Kenny's bullying isn't the only Pritchard problem we may have to deal with." Just then the telephone rang. Deirdre sprang to answer it.

"Hello? Oh, hello, Dad."

The room suddenly became very still.

"No, we're fine," Deirdre said into the phone. "Well, yes, some trees. And the shed was, like, pulverized! The phones were down for a while, so—yes, we went to the cellar, and if you ask me—"

They were silent as Deirdre listened.

"Wow, really? They're sure it was a tornado? Boy, and here I was just telling Hazel that . . . uh . . . that . . ." Deirdre's voice trailed off.

"Hmm? Oh, yeah . . . Hazel *and* Ned. Well, not long, of course. I mean, they really *just* got here. Practically. Dad, you know what? Charlotte's also here, and if you ask me, she probably should talk to you right now." Without waiting for an answer, Deirdre held out the phone to Charlotte.

Charlotte looked around the room. "Let me guess. You didn't call him to say Hazel and Ned were here."

Nobody answered. Hazel looked at her plate.

Charlotte took the phone.

"Seamus, hi. Everybody is fine, and the place is still standing," she said. "But we've been having a bit of trouble with the phones.

"Why don't we talk first, and I'll put them on after," she said following a pause. Then she made a shooing motion toward the door.

"Out," she whispered. "All of you. But don't go far."

All the cousins bolted for the porch. Charlotte closed the screen door and then the heavy wooden door as well. Now nothing of the phone conversation could be overheard. Hazel surveyed the grounds. The sun was shining cheerfully, making the rain-soaked lawn sparkle. It was turning into a beautiful day. Except . . . what if Uncle Seamus didn't want them there? What if he was telling Charlotte right now that they had to go? An involuntary shiver ran through her body.

"Are you cold?" asked Deirdre, concerned. "Is your wrist hurting?"

"No, I'm okay, although I would like to get out of these pajamas. It's just . . ." Hazel tried not to sound too worried. "Do you think your dad will be mad?"

"At you guys?" asked Mark. "No way. But he might not be thrilled with us."

"I guess we should have called him as soon as you arrived," Matt said.

"Maybe the storm was a blessing in disguise," said Deirdre. "Dad sounded pretty worried at first. He heard on the news a tornado really did touch down near here—just on the American side of the river. So he's got to be relieved we're okay. Maybe that will take the edge off things."

"Oh, yeah. He'll be in a fine mood," said Matt with a touch of sarcasm. "Until he hears about Hazel's wrist and our wild goose chase through the secret tunnel."

"What wild goose chase?" Mark asked.

"But the sprain isn't serious, and anyway, that's not your fault," Hazel protested, her words tumbling over Matt's.

"And Charlotte's positive it's not broken," added Deirdre.

"Helloooo!" Mark waved his long, skinny arms in Deirdre's face. "Will one of you tell me what's going on? What secret tunnel?"

Before anyone could answer, the door opened and Charlotte reappeared. "Hazel? Ned? Your uncle would like to speak with you both. Don't worry—he won't bite."

Hazel took a deep breath and walked into the

kitchen, Ned following closely behind her.

Uncle Seamus wasn't upset. He listened without interrupting as Hazel and Ned recounted their tale, and when it was his turn to speak, Uncle Seamus's voice was warm and friendly and, most of all, reassuring. It sounded a good deal like their father's voice, only slower and more ponderous.

"The most important thing is that you are both safe and at Land's End," Uncle Seamus said. "I'm very much looking forward to seeing the two of you, and if not for the situation with your father, I would leave this court tomorrow and head straight for the island."

"But I thought the case you were working on was really big," said Ned.

"The fun part is mostly over now," Uncle Seamus said with a low chuckle. "I can leave the rest to my associates."

Fun? Hazel had never thought of law as fun.

"So I thought I would head to Istanbul on the first available flight," their uncle was saying. "I just have to consult a few colleagues and make some calls first. You don't happen to know where Frankie was planning to stay in Istanbul, do you?"

"No," Hazel replied. "But you might check with Monsieur Gentil, our neighbor back home. She may have called and told him."

"An excellent suggestion," Uncle Seamus said. Ned

gave him the phone number. There was a pause.

"Now, children," Uncle Seamus said slowly, "I know you must have a great many questions. But please be patient awhile longer. I can't explain things over the telephone, and I think we'll agree that the priority is to secure your father's release from prison and his safe return home."

"Definitely," Hazel said. "But—"

"I'll return to Land's End as quickly as I can," Uncle Seamus said. "I promise that when I get home, I'll answer every question you wish to ask—about your parents, about the entire Frump clan. I'll tell your father this when I see him. There are to be *no more secrets* in this family. Do you understand?"

"Yes," Hazel answered, and somehow, without meaning to, added, "sir."

"Okay," agreed Ned.

"Good. Now please give my love to your cousins," Uncle Seamus said. "I'd love to speak to everyone, but I simply don't have time right now. As soon as it can be arranged, I'll return with your father, rest assured."

Hazel saw Ned smile. She felt the corners of her mouth turning up too.

"In the meantime, try to stay out of trouble. Stay clear of Clive Pritchard and any of his associates, including Kenny," Uncle Seamus ordered. "The burglary of your apartment has certain aspects I find . . . disturbing. Clearing everything out of your father's study, for example, was needlessly dramatic. In any case, if you think of anything else I should know, the children have my cell phone number."

After Hazel and Ned hung up, they returned to the porch, where their cousins were engrossed in a conversation that ceased immediately.

"Where's Charlotte?" Hazel asked.

"Sick goose," Mark answered. "But she'll be back later."

"What's the deal with Charlotte—is she Uncle Seamus's girlfriend?" Ned asked.

"No, she's our cousin, silly," Deirdre said.

"Your cousin too," Oliver said.

"So she's a Frump?" Ned asked.

Mark appeared to choke on air and began coughing. Matt thumped him on the back.

"Oh, you know how confusing family trees are," he said. "We're all related somehow . . . but never mind Charlotte. How did it go with Dad?"

Hazel looked at Ned. He nodded.

"First of all: You were right," she said. "Uncle Seamus wasn't upset with us, even when we told him everything."

"You told him everything?" Deirdre echoed.

Ned nodded solemnly.

"Now I guess we'd better tell you." Hazel sighed.

When Hazel and Ned had finished, they sat back, exhausted, and waited. But no one spoke. Hazel's eyes met Ned's. Were their cousins upset that Ned and Hazel had put them in danger?

"So your friend Frankie is over there right now, trying to help your father," Mark said finally.

Hazel and Ned nodded.

"And is Dad on his way to Istanbul?" Deirdre asked.

"Yup," answered Ned.

"Well," Mark said, "maybe we could help you figure out what's going on with the Pritchards and the painting and everything. What do you think?"

"Great," Hazel replied. "Where should we start?"

"Definitely with the painting your father gave you," Deirdre said.

Mark shook his head. "No, let's go check out that painting you saw in Clive's shop, the one Ned said looked like a Cafazzo."

"We're supposed to keep away from the Pritchards, remember?" said Oliver. "We should start with the websites."

Hazel could see the excitement she felt reflected in her cousins' eyes.

"Let's put everything together in one place," Matt said. "Like when you study for a test. Notes, the painting, that newspaper clipping—everything. Mark, we'll use your room. You've got the best computer."

"Aye, aye sir," Mark said in a mocking tone.

Half an hour later, they had each examined the painting carefully, turning it over and over, and all anyone could agree on was that the castle did look very much like Land's End. The newspaper clipping also proved useless. Ned searched again for the websites that had extolled the virtues of Paolo Cafazzo, but again came up empty-handed.

Things didn't start looking up until Ned produced the list he'd begun on the train, with the names he'd remembered from the missing websites, and Hazel found the page she'd torn from the notepad on Colin Frump's desk.

As six pairs of eyes scrutinized the scraps of paper, Deirdre let out a yelp.

"Oh! They're anagrams!" she said. "Don't you see it? Wow, I guess it's just like one of those puzzle things, you know, those inkblots where you have to stare at something a long time and then it just turns into something else."

"What do you mean, anagrams?" Oliver asked.

"A professor, a doctor, and a Ph.D. That's all sort of the same thing. So take away the word *professor* and substitute *Ph.D*. What do you get?"

She grabbed a blank sheet of paper from Mark's desk. In big block letters she wrote:

CRITIC REVA L. PH.D.

And below it:

LEVI TRICCAR PH.D.

And finally:

DR. CHIP VILECART

"Don't you see? Each name uses the same fourteen letters, just in different arrangements."

"Could that mean all those websites and all that stuff about Paolo Cafazzo was written by *one* guy?" Ned asked.

"Ah, but which guy?" said Deirdre. The smile on her face suggested she was enjoying everyone's confusion.

"You *know* who did this?" Ned asked.

Deirdre took the paper again, and beneath the first three names, she added two more. She turned the paper around so that the others could see. Hazel felt a sudden chill, as if someone had switched on an air conditioner.

RICHARD C. PLEVIT
CLIVE PRITCHARD

"It's the same fourteen letters every time," Deirdre said.

"This guy is nuts," Ned said.

*N*ed was sure the anagrams proved that a criminally insane mastermind—a madman—was behind everything from the disappearing websites to Colin Frump's imprisonment. But the more the six cousins thought about it, the less sense anything made to anyone. Eventually, they agreed to take a break for the rest of the day and devoted their energies to tidying the lawns and orchards and collecting the garbage that had washed up on the beaches during the storm.

By nightfall, they were all ready to try again. The cousins built a giant bonfire down on the pebbly shore closest to the castle. To Hazel's surprise, they used old kindling and logs that had been stored inside instead of the brush they had piled nearby.

"Shouldn't we be burning all the branches that

came down in the storm, along with the bits and pieces of the shed?" Hazel asked.

"It would still be too wet," Matt replied. "But it'll be fine later in the summer. We've got big plans for Dad's birthday—a huge bonfire, fireworks. You'll see."

There was a warm feeling in the pit of Hazel's stomach. Matt was the cousin she felt the least sure of; he was the quieter, more serious of the twins, and of the four cousins he was definitely the one who seemed most wary of her and Ned. But now here he was, talking as if they'd all be together for the rest of summer vacation. He even sounded happy about it.

"Right. Time to figure out what Clive Pritchard is up to," said Mark, rubbing his hands together and looking expectantly around at the group.

"Speaking of Mr. Pritchard, are we sure he won't come back?" Oliver asked. As he spoke, the boy glanced over his shoulder into the growing darkness that surrounded their fire pit. But there was no sign of anyone.

"We've gone over this a dozen times," Deirdre said. "Even if he does come back, we don't know for sure that he's dangerous. I mean, I guess we know he's not a *good* guy, but . . ."

"His buddy Richard C. Plevit, he's dangerous, though," Ned reminded her. "He hurt Frankie."

That put a damper on the conversation. For a few minutes the only sounds anyone could hear were the crackle and hiss of the fire and, in the background, the gentle *shhh* of the waves lapping the shore. Hazel tore her gaze away from the leaping flames to look skyward. The stars were coming out.

"Anyway, as far as the whole anagram thing goes," Ned said, breaking the silence, "I guess we know that 'Clive Pritchard' *is* actually Clive Pritchard's real name."

"Yeah," Mark agreed. "We've lived on the island all our lives, so we know Clive Pritchard is who he says he is. He was born here. Maybe he uses aliases when he's not on the island, but when he's here, he can't hide. I mean, everyone knows him."

"So I suppose that means we can assume it's the people like Critic Reva L. who don't exist," Ned continued. "Unless they do exist, but they have made-up names."

"I guess that would make Clive Pritchard the evil mastermind," said Oliver, "if he gets to go around naming everyone else after himself."

"Pretty egotistical, if you ask me," Deirdre said.

"I wonder what Richard C. Plevit's *real* name is," Hazel said.

"*I* wonder what Clive Pritchard was doing here at Land's End," Matt said. "After everything you've told us, it's obvious he wasn't here to complain about the basketball game. And I did think he was following us, at first. But if he had been chasing us, he would have ended up on the beach like we did. I think maybe he *wanted* us to run away."

"To scare us?" Hazel asked.

Matt just shrugged. Reliving their flight through the tunnels, Hazel recalled the moment when she had wanted to turn right, but Matt had ordered them to go left. Hazel sat up a little straighter.

"What if he wasn't trying to scare us exactly, so much as scare us off? You know what I mean? Like, what if he was trying to keep us away from something?" Hazel asked. "Matt, you said you never go into those tunnels, and nobody but Uncle Seamus and you even knew they were there. But Clive Pritchard obviously knew about them! What if he's been using them for something? What if he hid something there, something he didn't want us to find?"

"We should go back in there and poke around a little," Mark said.

"Tomorrow might be good," Oliver said in a small voice. "It's getting kind of dark now."

"Well, it's going to be dark down there no matter when we go, silly," Deirdre said. "But tomorrow sounds like a good idea. I'm exhausted."

"It has been a pretty long day," Matt said.

Hazel suppressed a sigh of frustration. The more

she thought about it, the more she was convinced there must be something in those tunnels. That pull she'd felt—it couldn't just be a coincidence. Did they really have to wait until morning to investigate?

"In the meantime, isn't there anything else we can do?" Ned asked. Hazel could tell from his voice that he shared her impatience.

"We could try to reach that Inspector O'Toole," Mark suggested. "I'm not sure where in Europe Interpol is based, but wherever it is, it'll be in a time zone six hours or so ahead of ours. If we stay up late enough, it'll be morning there and we can call."

"I don't know if anyone there will take a bunch of kids seriously," Matt said, "but I guess we could try."

They sat in silence for a while, staring at the flames. Looking at everyone's faces, Hazel could see they were discouraged. They had so many questions and so few answers. As before, Ned was the first to break the silence.

"So—back in the city, Clive Pritchard was driving a Ferrari," Ned commented. "That makes him a pretty rich man. How'd he make his money?"

Before anyone could answer, they heard the sound of footsteps crunching along the gravel shore. Straining her eyes to see who was approaching in the darkness, Hazel made out a figure. She just had time to think that the person didn't look large enough to be

Richard C. Plevit when a woman's voice rang out: "Yoo-hoo, Frumps—I came to ask if I could keep the truck another day or two!"

It was Charlotte. As she drew nearer, the bonfire cast a rosy glow over her cheerful grin. She reached into her purse and pulled out a bag of marshmallows. "I grabbed these from your kitchen when I saw the bonfire."

For the next several minutes, Mark and Oliver showed Ned how to select a roasting stick from the sodden pile of fallen tree branches and prune away any unnecessary twigs.

Finally, Matt cleared his throat. "We figure somehow Clive Pritchard has to be behind Uncle Colin's arrest, but we don't really know how or why. Any ideas?"

Charlotte poked the embers nearest her and frowned. "No. There's some sort of bad blood between them, but whatever it was, it happened long ago. I don't know the details. But we do know this wouldn't be the first time Clive Pritchard tangled with the law."

"Really?" the twins chorused in unison.

"Yeah. You're all too young to have heard about it, but he was sort of the local bad boy when he was younger. It was a shame really, because he had so much talent."

"What kind of talent?" Hazel asked.

"Oh, he was a very talented artist," Charlotte said. "But he never wanted to work at anything. I remember he was always getting into trouble for drawing these portraits—caricatures really—of the teachers at high school. They were very good. He captured their faces perfectly, but he'd always ruin it by adding something disrespectful. You'd start to laugh at first, and then you'd look more closely at the drawing and see how cruel it really was, and you'd . . . just wish you'd never even seen it."

"Was his family rich?" Ned asked.

"No, not at all," Charlotte answered. "Why do you ask?"

"Well, if he didn't inherit money, then somewhere along the way he figured out how to make a ton of it," Ned said. "Does anyone know how he did it?"

"It was from some telemarketing business," Charlotte said. "I think it actually got into legal trouble. He had some kind of fraud or scam going on. But that was years ago. I can't remember if Clive was ever charged with anything, although I think perhaps his partner went to jail."

"Did anything ever get published about it in the local papers?" asked Hazel.

"You mean back then? I think so." Charlotte frowned. "I think it also came up again in a magazine article a few years later . . . when the government was talking about cracking down on white-collar crime."

Hazel looked at Ned. But he and Oliver had their heads together and were whispering.

"It's a good thing you dropped by, Charlotte," Mark said.

"Well, I meant to take Hazel to a doctor this afternoon, but I got too busy. We'll go tomorrow, okay?"

Before Hazel could answer, Ned and Oliver got to their feet.

"Let's go, you guys," Ned said.

"Where to?" asked Deirdre.

"We need to get back on the computer." Ned grinned. "Some of those articles are bound to turn up on the internet, and we have way more leads to follow now."

"Okay, okay—but safety first," Matt said. "Let's put this fire out."

The embers sizzled as the children emptied buckets of lake water onto the flames. Hazel turned her head away to avoid choking on the smoke. Matt's words echoed in her head: *safety first*. Not a bad idea.

15

It was lucky that Mark had such a big room; as tired as everyone was, nobody wanted to be left out of the search. Mark unceremoniously dumped piles of magazines onto the floor so that Charlotte could sit in the most comfortable chair. As the glossy pages slid past her feet, Hazel noticed that most of their titles related to food in some way.

"*Gourmet/Gourmand*," she read aloud. "*Eat Something! Chocolate Today*. . . . It sounds like you're already on your way to becoming a chef."

Mark grinned. "Oh, who knows?" he said. "Maybe I'll become a detective."

Ned and Oliver had settled the question of which search engine to use and were busily experimenting with different combinations of words. Typing *Clive*

Pritchard came back with too many hits. But once they started entering phrases such as *Clive Pritchard telemarketing* and *Clive Pritchard scam fraud,* the boys hit the jackpot. The first place their nemesis popped up was on a list started by a teenager in California, who claimed her family received fifty phone calls every day from telemarketers.

"It's impossible to concentrate with everyone breathing down our necks," Ned said as they all crowded around to read the next big discovery, a university student's analysis of telemarketers' methods. (Clive Pritchard figured prominently.)

Oliver agreed. "From now on, as soon as we get a hit, I'm printing out a copy of whatever it is and moving on," he told the others. "You guys can divide them up. Ned and me will just keep searching for stuff and printing it out."

"Ned and *I*," corrected Deirdre.

"No, better let Oliver handle it," Ned said. "He's pretty good with this stuff."

Deirdre rolled her eyes. "Hilarious, Ned. Just give me the printout."

The next hour or so passed with Ned and Oliver at the computer while Charlotte and the others spread out in a circle on the floor, reading and passing around the printouts. As Ned and Oliver became more successful in their searches and more selective about the material they chose to print, Hazel began to lose herself in the reading. Several hours passed, the silence in the room punctuated by outbursts of "Hey, take a look at this!" or "Wait until you read this bit."

Eventually, Ned and Oliver announced they were too tired to go on, and everyone agreed they already had more than enough information.

"Okay," Charlotte said as she sorted the printed pages into neat stacks and laid them out across the worn Persian carpet. "Let's see what we've got."

What they had was an odd collection of pages culled from newspaper and magazine articles, academic research, chat rooms, personal websites, and one or two blogs.

"The internet is one strange universe," Mark said. "There's stuff here from five or six years ago and stuff from yesterday. And who knows how much of it is true?"

"Well, we can safely say we now know a *few* things for sure," Charlotte said. "For example, Clive Pritchard seems to have owned or partly owned a whole series of companies over the years, and most of them have gotten into trouble with the law."

"Yeah, but he generally gets off with a slap on the wrist," Matt said in disgust. "And then he just disappears for a while and resurfaces later, with some other company."

"It looks like he scams new victims each time," Deirdre said, slowly leafing through one of the piles. "But I think he also doubles back and rips off the same people over and over—only they don't seem to catch on. The same people who sign on to complain about being swindled by Clive's first company, the Fazza Co.? They show up the next year complaining about being ripped off by the Opal Company, which Clive Pritchard also started."

"Some people never learn, I guess," Mark said. "What's that saying? If it sounds like something's too good to be true, it probably is?"

"Or how about: There's a sucker born every minute," Matt replied, shaking his head. "Pritchard seems to run a lot of get-rich-quick scams, mostly by suggesting he has some kind of insider information."

"He gets around a lot too," Hazel said. "I mean, for somebody who's so busy starting up company after company, he spends a lot of time at parties and charity fund-raisers."

"Yeah, so does his buddy. What's the guy's name?" Mark asked. "Paul something . . . Paul Fazza."

"That first company must have been named after him—the Fazza Co.," Deirdre said. "He's some kind of art collector and patron of the arts. They're always showing up at galas together and stuff."

"With a name like Fazza . . . is he Italian?" Oliver asked.

"No, I think I read somewhere he's from Turkey," Matt replied.

"Hey. That's gotta be more than a coincidence, with Uncle Colin being in a Turkish prison," Mark said.

"Yeah, but we still don't know what it all means," Ned said with a sigh.

"And on that note, I really think we should call it quits for tonight," said Charlotte. She was half sitting, half lying across the end of Mark's bed, her eyes closed. "I've still got to drive home. But it's probably good we did all this now—they were saying in the village that the wind did so much damage, they're expecting more trees to come down. The phone service is going to be off and on for a couple of days while they do repairs.

"See you tomorrow, Frumps?" she said.

Everyone nodded except Deirdre, who had fallen asleep on the rug.

"I'll come down with you. I think I should lock up for the night," Matt said, following Charlotte out of the room.

"Listen, I know we should all go to bed, and I promise to get out of your room really soon," Hazel told Mark. "But there's one thing I want to check first."

"Sure," her cousin agreed, although he couldn't stifle a massive yawn. "Like what?"

"It's all the charity balls and parties and stuff," Hazel said. "I'm just wondering why Clive Pritchard would waste his time with them. I mean, at first I thought he was trying to rebuild his reputation. But if he cares so much what people think of him, why keep ripping them off with the telemarketing companies? He doesn't exactly act like somebody who's trying to turn over a new leaf."

"So what's your idea?" Oliver demanded.

"Can I use the computer for a few minutes?" Hazel said in response. "I know it would probably go faster if somebody with two good hands did the typing, but I just want to see for myself. Okay?"

The three boys shrugged and stood back as Hazel settled herself in front of the monitor. It took her a few minutes; Hazel hadn't spent as much time searching the internet as the younger boys, and her injury didn't help. But by the time Matt reappeared, she had printed out what she needed.

"Okay. Now, compare the names in *these* printouts to the ones we already read—about the parties and the fund-raisers," Hazel said, handing copies of news reports to the four boys.

"These are all articles about stolen art and jewelry," Mark said in a puzzled voice, "all stuff that was taken from homes and museums across Canada, the United States, and Europe."

"Exactly," Hazel said. "But look at the names of the people who had their stuff stolen and look at the names of the people who attended those parties with Clive Pritchard."

The boys studied the pages. Oliver rubbed his eyes as if he could barely keep them open.

"I get it," Matt said. "Anywhere from a few days to a few months after Clive shows up at one of these parties, the host or hostess is robbed. . . . Or one of the other party guests is burgled."

Hazel nodded. "And lots of times that Paul Fazza guy turns up at those parties too," she added. "I think they're more than business partners. I think they're partners in crime."

"Wow," Oliver said, impressed. "So they'll steal from anybody."

"Including our dad," Ned observed. "I'd bet money they're the ones who burgled our apartment and cleaned out Dad's study."

"I'm still confused, though," Matt said.

"Join the club!" said Mark. "The whole thing's confusing. I mean, okay, so Clive Pritchard and this guy, Paul Fazza, are ripping people off with the tele-marketing businesses. And maybe robbing rich folks too—or just organizing the burglaries. But how does that fit in with Ned's project on that artist, Paolo Cafazzo, and the websites that disappeared and the painting Hazel has and Uncle Colin going to jail?"

"You left out Richard C. Plevit," Matt added. "Where does he fit in?"

Deirdre mumbled in her sleep and rolled over. The carpet had left a red mark on her cheek.

"What did she just say?" Hazel asked.

"I think she said *anagrams*," Oliver answered.

A light switched on in Hazel's head. Reaching for one of the stacks of paper the boys had printed out, she began riffling through it furiously.

"Anyone got a pen?" she asked. "Or a pencil—anything? Deirdre may be able to do this in her head, but I can't. I have to see the letters on paper."

"What are you talking about?" Mark asked, handing her a pen. But Hazel was too busy scribbling to reply right away.

"Anagrams," said Hazel after a moment. She set down the pen with a flourish. "Check this out: Clive Pritchard's first company was called the Fazza Co., after his partner, Paul Fazza."

"So?" Oliver asked.

"Well, if you rearrange the letters in *Fazza Co.*, you get *Cafazzo*, and then *Paul* in Italian is *Paolo*, right? So that makes *Paolo Cafazzo*!"

"I hate these anagrams," Matt announced.

"There's more," said Hazel. "After the Fazza Co., Clive opens something called the Opal Company and starts selling worthless 'gems' to people over the phone."

"I don't see any anagram there," Mark confessed.

"Then take another look at this gossip column," Hazel said, pointing. "The one that talks about Clive Pritchard supposedly naming the Opal Company after a former girlfriend, someone named Opal Fazzoa."

"If you rearrange the letters in the name *Opal Fazzoa Co.*, do you get *Paolo Cafazzo?*" guessed Ned.

"Bingo!" Hazel said triumphantly.

"I still don't get it, though," Mark said. "Do *any* of these names belong to real people? Is there really a Paolo Cafazzo, a Paul Fazza, or an Opal Fazzoa?"

"I'm pretty sure at this point that Paolo Cafazzo isn't real," Ned said. He had returned to the computer and was tapping away furiously at the keyboard. "I bet they give each other name anagrams—Pritchard uses Cafazzo and Fazza uses Plevit. So Clive Pritchard is Paolo Cafazzo. He probably took his artistic talents and put them to use creating this phony Romantic artist. He's not just greedy, he's crazy! I don't even think it's about the money anymore. I think he just likes making fools out of people."

"What are you looking for?" asked Hazel.

"I'm looking for Richard C. Plevit," Ned

answered. "I think all along, this has been about two men—two greedy, crazy men—who like to make up aliases out of anagrams 'cause they think they're clever. Somewhere on the internet there's got to be a photograph and a name . . . aha!"

"Did you really just say *aha!*?" Mark asked, shaking his head.

"I'm entitled," Ned said. "This is an *aha!* if there ever was one. Take a look!"

Hazel, Oliver, and the twins leaned forward to peer at the computer screen. A grainy photograph of a heavyset man with a strikingly large bulbous nose swam before their eyes. Hazel could just make out the jagged scar she'd glimpsed in the gallery.

"That's him," she said. "That's Richard C. Plevit!"

Scanning the text that accompanied it, Hazel read that he was Paul Fazza, an entrepreneur who had grown up in Turkey and now lived in Montreal. He was described as a patron of the arts and a collector of Romantic paintings.

"So Richard C. Plevit is really Paul Fazza," Matt said hesitantly, as if half expecting someone to correct him.

"Right," Mark said.

"So that means there are two bad guys: Clive Pritchard and his accomplice, Paul Fazza, also known as Plevit," Oliver said.

Hazel and Ned nodded.

"Well, that explains everything," said Mark, his voice dripping with sarcasm.

Hazel didn't know whether to laugh or cry. Mark was right; there were still so many unanswered questions.

"Look, it's two o'clock in the morning," Matt said. "We could stay up until dawn trying to figure out what those guys are up to and how Uncle Colin got mixed up in it. But I think we'd be better off getting some sleep."

Deirdre was sleeping so soundly, Mark had to sling her over his shoulder and carry her to her room. The others stumbled down the halls.

Back in her room, Hazel expected to find sleep the moment her head hit the pillow—maybe even before. Yet, tired as she was, sleep refused to come. Long after she had stopped counting yawns, she was still wide awake.

Tossing back the covers in frustration, Hazel sat up and peered outside. The breeze from the open window sent a tiny shiver down her back. The moon was almost full and cast a cold, glittering path across the lake toward the tiny island. Hazel's eyes followed the moonlight to where the Martello tower and the surrounding pines should have appeared as inky blobs.

But bright lights blazed from the tower.

Deirdre was in mid snore when Hazel burst through the door.

"Wake up!" Hazel shook her cousin by the shoulders. "There's someone in the tower!"

"What? What tower? *This* tower?" Deirdre asked, squinting up at Hazel.

"No, the one on the little island," Hazel said, gesturing toward the window. "The Martello tower."

"Probably just kids goofing around," Deirdre said. She yawned and lay back against the pillows. "We can report it to the police tomorrow."

"Are you crazy? You can't just go back to sleep." Hazel yanked on Deirdre's arm. "That tower is the last place I saw Richard C. Plevit. I mean Paul Fazza. Oh, whatever his name is—you know, Clive Pritchard's accomplice. It's got to be them."

But Deirdre had rolled onto her stomach and bunched her pillow over her head to block Hazel's voice.

"Fine, get your beauty rest," Hazel said. "I'll get the others; *they* won't want to miss this."

But just a few doors away from Ned and Oliver's room, a sudden thought struck Hazel and she stopped in mid stride. What if there was another way to the island? What if *that* was where Clive Pritchard had gone after they left the tunnels? What if he had turned right instead of left, and ended up at the island?

The instant the thought occurred to her, Hazel knew it was true. The tunnel *must* lead to the tower. She would stake her life on it. She'd wondered whether Clive Pritchard was hiding something in the tunnels, but now she knew it had to be in the Martello tower. Only, since he knew the Frumps had discovered the tunnels, he'd come back, under cover of darkness, to clear away whatever he'd hidden.

She was running now, and her mind was racing faster than her feet could carry her. He couldn't use the tunnels—at least not the part that led into the castle cellar. He couldn't take the risk they'd hear him. So how had Clive Pritchard gotten there? And how would he take things off the island? He must have a boat. He, or Paul Fazza, could have hidden a boat around the far side of the island, where the trees towered over a high slope. They could have watched until the Frumps' bonfire was extinguished, waited even until most of the lights in the castle were switched off, then gone to work.

Hazel was in the cellar before she realized she had no flashlight. It had been one thing to enter the musty passageway with four others and a flashlight. It was quite another thing to go in alone, with nothing, not even a candle or some matches.

But as she hesitated by the door to the box room, Hazel remembered how Deirdre had spied the cigarette butt on the floor and then the lighter on the old trunk.

"Please let this thing still work," Hazel whispered aloud as her hand closed around the metal lighter. It was blanketed by a thick layer of dust, but when she flicked it on, a tiny flame spurted out; she fumbled and almost dropped it in her excitement.

"Thank you," Hazel murmured.

Just possessing the lighter cheered Hazel immensely, even though she had no way of knowing how much lighter fluid was left. But as she began making her way down the dusty tunnel, she found her eyes slowly growing accustomed to the darkness.

It seemed to Hazel that she reached the place where the tunnel diverged a little sooner than she had when she was with the others. But then Matt hadn't been hurrying at the beginning, and tonight Hazel was determined to move as quickly as possible. She had to reach the tower before Clive Pritchard or Paul Fazza escaped.

Resolutely pushing all thoughts of insects and spiders to the back of her mind, Hazel set off down the right-hand tunnel. She found herself slowing a little at first. But this tunnel proved easier than the one that had led the children to the beach; it was wider and, within a minute or two, it was taller as well. Presently, Hazel became aware that the gradual downhill slant of the passageway was growing steeper.

"I must be going under the lake," she said, hoping the sound of her own voice would reassure her. But her whispered phrase echoed eerily back to her, growing louder before it died away.

The tunnel suddenly widened again, and Hazel could make out a thin ribbon of light just ahead, running along the ground. As she drew closer, she flicked the lighter and realized the ribbon she'd glimpsed was light escaping from under the bottom of a small oak door set in a stone wall. She had come to the end of the tunnel.

Hazel put a hand on the door and listened. She could hear nothing from the other side. Feeling around for a way to open it, her hands closed on a cold metal knob. No dust, Hazel observed. Someone had come through this door recently. But when she took a deep breath and turned the knob, nothing happened. She put her shoulder to the door and pushed; still, it refused to budge. She flicked the lighter again. The door was no taller than she was, and just at eye level there was an old-fashioned keyhole with a long embellished key protruding from the lock. The key turned easily in her hands, and she heard the latch give way. Hazel twisted the knob and pushed.

She was standing at the entrance to a large, round room encircled by walls of rough-hewn stone. The floor was formed from the same hard-packed earth as the tunnels, but the low ceiling was fashioned from wide planks of wood laid across beams the size and shape of massive tree trunks. A steep, narrow staircase led to a trapdoor directly above her head. This had to be the Martello tower.

The room was completely empty. If anything had been hidden here, it had already been removed. Yet judging by the muffled sounds of voices and the creaking of the boards above her head, it was clear that several men were still hard at work upstairs. Holding her breath, Hazel crept toward the staircase and settled herself on the bottom step to listen.

"We should have cleared this place out long ago,

Pritchard." It was the voice of the man Hazel had heard threaten Frankie.

"Relax, Fazza," said a voice that had to belong to Clive Pritchard. "A couple more hours and we're out of here. Everything will be loaded onto the boat. No worries."

"I do worry," replied the other man. "You never know when to quit, that's your problem. You had to invent that ridiculous Paolo Cafazzo just to get back at Frump."

"If he'd believed in my fakes, we could have been huge," Pritchard retorted. "An endorsement from Colin Frump could have made us millions."

"You just wanted the satisfaction of conning him. How many times do I have to tell you: it's about making a score, not settling one. But now he's taken our Cafazzo—probably to the cops."

Hazel had heard enough. The men clearly didn't know any more than she did. While Uncle Seamus was figuring things out in Istanbul, it probably wouldn't hurt if Hazel could turn Fazza and Pritchard over to the police.

But for that, she'd need help.

Hazel was backing down the steps as quietly as she could, when she heard Fazza ask, "What about the cellar? Did we get everything out?"

Hazel's heart skipped a beat. Maybe two.

She didn't wait for Clive Pritchard's answer. Hazel scampered across the room and escaped through the tunnel door, pulling it shut behind her. With trembling fingers she reached up and turned the key in the lock as heavy footsteps thudded down the stairs she had perched on just moments ago.

Hazel froze. If she ran now, would he hear her? She didn't want the men to know they'd been discovered. Leaning against the tunnel wall, eyes fixed on the door she *hoped* she had just locked, Hazel willed herself to remain calm. She clamped her uninjured hand over her nose and mouth to stifle the sound of her breathing. Hazel didn't move until she heard the footsteps retreating up the stairs. Then she bolted, running as fast as she could in the darkness to the safety of the castle.

When Hazel emerged from the cellar, out of breath, heart pounding, she heard voices coming from the kitchen. Ned and the four Frump cousins were overjoyed to see her. Deirdre had jolted awake, minutes after Hazel left. Finding Hazel's room empty, she'd roused the others.

"So where did you go?" Deirdre asked, her voice cracking. "Did I dream it, or did you say something about going to the tower?"

Hazel filled them in as quickly as she could. "And they're still there," she finished. "But they said something about a boat. We've got to find some way to trap them on the island or keep them here until we can get the police!"

Matt picked up the phone. "It's dead," he said, his face pale.

"And our truck's still over at Charlotte's," Oliver added.

Hazel felt her heart sink. They couldn't let Clive Pritchard escape, not now.

"Well, we're not totally helpless," Mark said, rubbing his hands together with a look of mischief. "For example, Matt, I seem to recall a rather mean trick you played years ago when Gordon Paige was showing off with his new boat."

Hazel didn't understand, but she could see that Matt did.

Deirdre let out a whoop. "Omigosh, Mark! That's brilliant," she cried. "Hazel, Matt once stranded this guy on that very island by taking a little piece out of the engine on his boat. He could do it again, couldn't you, Matt?"

Hazel stared at her cousin in disbelief. *Matt* had done that? It sounded more like something Mark would have done.

"In the meantime, I'll go for help," Deirdre offered. "It won't take me more than twenty minutes or so to get to Charlotte's."

"Go then," Mark said. "And tell Charlotte to get the police over here as soon as possible and to alert the coast guard, too."

Deirdre nodded and disappeared out the door.

Mark turned to Matt. "If you're going to sneak over there and disable their boat engine, you'll need a distraction here onshore," he said. "I'll give you ten minutes' head start, then I'll start setting off those fireworks we bought for Dad's birthday."

"I don't know . . . they still could decide to swim for it before Deirdre manages to bring help," Matt said. But he rose from the table anyway.

"Hey, what about us?" Ned asked.

"Uh . . . you two stay by the phones and keep checking for a dial tone," Mark said. "The instant that sucker's working, you call nine-one-one."

From their expressions, Hazel could see Ned and Oliver were unimpressed by the role assigned to them. But she was starting to get an idea herself.

"What about me?" she asked evenly.

"Kiddo, you've had enough adventures for one night," Mark said. "You're exhausted. Stay here and keep an eye on the squirts."

Without waiting for a reply, he was gone. Hazel could hear him holler to Matt as he headed down the hallway: "I'm going to set the fireworks off from the lookout tower, so they'll be sure to see 'em. Better get paddling, bro. The first one's going off in ten minutes . . . nine minutes and fifty-nine seconds . . . nine minutes and fifty-eight seconds. . . ."

Matt surveyed the younger boys' glum faces. "Sorry, kids. Take care of Hazel," was all he said before he too disappeared.

Hazel let silence reign in the kitchen for a few moments.

"You don't really think we're just going to sit here, do you?" she asked. "Matt's right. The crooks could just swim to shore . . . unless we stop them first."

"But how?" Ned asked.

"I'm thinking about the NIDS," Hazel said. She was smiling broadly now. "The original one's in my room. You guys didn't happen to make another, did you?"

"**I** think Oliver made the right decision, staying behind to dial nine-one-one if the phones start working again," Ned whispered.

Hazel looked more closely at her brother. Oliver had supplied her with a flashlight, and now it was easy to see the nervousness in Ned's eyes. Tiny beads of sweat had formed on his brow, even though it was cool in the tunnel.

"You don't have to come in with me," Hazel said. "You can just hand me the stink bombs and wait here by the door. You can be in charge of slamming the door shut after I get back, and locking it."

Ned squared his shoulders. "It doesn't matter anyway because I'm coming with you. We started this together and we're going to finish it together."

Hazel squeezed her brother's arm.

"I can't think of anyone else I'd rather have with me," she said. Then she cocked her head to one side. "Unless maybe I could have one of those guys from the martial arts movies who kick through stone walls with their bare feet and smash metal pipes with their hands."

Ned laughed. "Maybe we should get going before we miss everything," he said. "By my watch, Mark's probably already set off the first firework."

Hazel turned the key and pushed open the door. The round cellar room was as empty as she'd left it, but the trapdoor above their heads was now open. Hazel recoiled, pushing Ned back against the wall. But the tower was deserted. The men were gone.

"Hey! Watch it!" Ned hissed. "I told you, the NIDS is very sensitive. We don't want to set them off accidentally. We'll only have between five and ten seconds to get away before the smell overwhelms us."

"Sorry," Hazel said. She put her foot on the lowest step of the staircase and began to climb. "Just how bad are these things?" she whispered.

"Well, the smell is like rotten eggs mixed with vomit, and it'll make the air unbearable for a good six to eight hours," Ned said in a low voice. "If it gets on your skin, it'll last even longer, and washing just seems to make it worse. Oh—and there's a particularly nasty side effect I haven't been able to get rid of. If it gets in your eyes, there's this horrible itching and pain that takes a long time to go away."

Hazel stared at her brother for a long moment. "All I can say is I'm glad you're on *my* side." Then she turned and continued her climb.

Hazel didn't entirely trust the silence in the tower. When the moment came to poke her head through the trapdoor, she found it took all her resolve not to flinch or close her eyes.

But there was nothing on the dirty wooden floor except some scraps of cardboard and a roll of packing tape. She scrambled up the rest of the stairs, beckoning to Ned to follow.

A heavy wooden door leading to the outside was slightly ajar. Hugging the far wall, Hazel could see a stone staircase that led to an upper floor; it traced a semicircle around half the room as it climbed. Hazel stared at it. There was something familiar about those stairs. In fact, now that she was aboveground, there was something familiar about this whole place.

But she had no time to think about it. Ned was dragging her across the room to one of the tall arched windows that looked out over the lake. Showers of pink, gold, and brilliant white were raining down from the castle's lookout tower. Mark had proved as good as his word.

"I hope this is the distraction Matt needs," Ned muttered.

Just then they heard shouts from outside. Hurrying to the door, the siblings peered through the opening. The fireworks were behind them, but their bursts of light, combined with an almost-full moon, were strong enough to illuminate the little clearing surrounding the tower. Hazel could see that just beyond the trees a large boat was moored to a dock. At least three men were moving around on it.

There was a loud splash, and both children heard Paul Fazza yell, "Stop him! He tried to do something to my boat—don't let him get away!"

Hazel pushed the tower door open wider and stepped outside. Her brother followed. "I can't see—did they get Matt?" she asked.

Ned peered through the trees then pointed triumphantly. "I see him! He's in the canoe, paddling away from the island!"

"I wish we knew whether he sabotaged the boat before they spotted him," Hazel said.

"I don't think he had enough time," Ned replied. "We'd better get out of here before they spot us."

"I guess," Hazel said, frowning.

Ned was already at the bottom of the cellar stairs by the time Hazel reached the trapdoor. And then she heard it: the engine on the yacht was coming to life. It made a spluttering sound and then another. Hazel froze. She didn't want Clive Pritchard and his accomplices to get away. She also didn't want them using their boat to catch up to Matt's canoe.

"Ned," she said. "I need one of the NIDS."

Ned handed up the heavier of the two bags.

"Here's the deal. I'm going to go back out there and throw one onto the yacht," said Hazel.

"What about the other one?"

"How about we deliver that one to Clive Pritchard personally?" Hazel said.

Ned peered up at her, his eyes thoughtful. "It's tempting," he said. "But I think this last one should be for the tower, so they can't follow us into the tunnel."

That made the most sense, even though the image of Clive Pritchard covered in stink held a certain emotional appeal.

"Okay, good idea," Hazel said.

"What's a good idea, little girl?"

It was Clive Pritchard. Hazel slowly tore her eyes from Ned's frightened gaze and looked across to where the tower door was now wide open. The slender blond man was leaning against the door jamb, arms crossed. "Who are you talking to?" Clive Pritchard inquired in a silky voice. "Are you a friend of that young man out there? Is there another friend hiding downstairs, perhaps?"

Hazel kept her gaze fixed on Clive Pritchard, but she spoke to her brother in a low voice. "You go back the way we came and don't wait for me—I think I feel like going for a swim. But what we just talked about? We're still going to do it: both of us, on my count. I'm depending on you. Do you understand?"

Hazel risked darting a glance at Ned. Barely waiting for his nod, she took a step toward Clive Pritchard.

"Just what do you think you are up to, child?" Pritchard asked.

"On three," Hazel said quietly. "Throw hard and don't worry about me—just go. *One!*"

Hazel was moving toward Clive Pritchard now. She could feel her palms sweating and hoped she didn't drop the bomb prematurely.

"Two," she yelled. Then, as if she was on a basketball court, she feinted left. Clive Pritchard tried to block her, unfolding his arms and moving away from the door. At the last second, Hazel veered right, sped past Clive, and ran through the open door. Caught off guard by Hazel's sudden change of direction, Pritchard stumbled and almost fell.

Outside the tower, Hazel stopped abruptly and swung around to face the entrance. *"Three!"* she shouted as loudly as she could.

Hazel saw a small object fly up from the open

trapdoor. It smashed on the wooden floor. Clive Pritchard took a step toward the broken stink bomb; Hazel began backing away from the tower. Pritchard howled and fell to his knees, bringing his hands to his eyes. Hazel turned and ran as fast as she could, toward the boat.

Paul Fazza and another man were standing aboard the yacht. The noise of the still-sputtering engine masked the sound of Hazel's running feet and heavy breathing. They didn't notice her until she reached the rocky shore.

"Who are you?" Paul Fazza asked angrily. "What are you doing here?"

Before Hazel could answer, the air was split by unearthly howls. Even she turned to see what was making the sound. Clive Pritchard was stumbling down the hill toward them, his hands over his eyes.

"Help me, I'm dying," he screamed, before running headlong into a tree. Hazel winced.

"He's not dying," Hazel assured the two men, who were transfixed by the sight of Pritchard. He was now rolling on the ground, moaning and still clutching his eyes.

"But he does feel pretty bad," Hazel continued. "And so will you, if you try to use this boat."

With that, she hurled the remaining stink bomb onto the deck of the yacht. It should have been a dramatic moment, and it would have been, if the bomb had burst as it was supposed to. But instead it lay on the gleaming deck, looking about as threatening as a jar of applesauce.

"Oops," she muttered under her breath.

"What's this?" Paul Fazza asked, stooping to pick up the stink bomb.

"Let me see," demanded the other man, in a whiny tone that reminded Hazel of Kenny Pritchard.

The men were so intent on the stink bomb, they seemed to have forgotten about her and the moaning Clive Pritchard. Hazel peered at the water lapping at the rocky ledge she was standing on. She had no way of knowing the water's depth or whether there were more rocks below the surface, but she had no choice. With one eye on the bickering men, Hazel crouched down and removed her shoes. She took off the sling that had been supporting her injured wrist and stuck one foot into the black water. It was cold.

Hazel lowered herself quickly into the lake and began swimming away from the island. Several strokes later she heard a loud pop and the sound of shattering glass. She quickened her stroke.

"Agh, what is this? I can't see!" Paul Fazza yelled.

The Frumps had done it. They had trapped all three men—well and truly.

All Hazel had to worry about now was staying

afloat and making it to shore. But as the island receded behind her, Hazel realized the castle was much farther away than she'd thought. The waves were higher too, and unless she was mistaken, there was a current pulling her slightly off course. The glow of satisfaction she'd felt about capturing Pritchard and Fazza was fading fast. She couldn't feel her toes for the cold, and with her wrist injured, she couldn't use her strongest strokes. The best she could manage was an old-fashioned sidestroke.

Something bumped against her leg.

"Hazel! Grab my hand and I'll pull you up," Matt said.

It was easier said than done, but two long minutes later, a shivering Hazel was slumped in the bottom of the canoe. Mark draped a moth-eaten blanket over her shoulders. It took her a few more minutes to become fully aware that the canoe was being propelled toward shore by Matt, seated in the rear, and Mark, who was in the front.

"Hey, good fireworks," she mumbled through lips numbed by cold.

"Thanks," Mark replied. "But it sounds like you and Ned put on a pretty good show yourselves."

"Ned!" Hazel said, struggling to sit upright. "Is he okay? Did he make it back?"

"Yes," Matt answered. "He ran back through the

tunnels so fast, I don't think he stopped to breathe. He sent us to get you."

"Whoa." Mark stopped paddling and pointed to the shore. "They must have sent a launch from Frontenac."

"Yeah," Matt said. "I've never seen that many police officers on the island before."

18

Hazel listened as Mark and Matt walked several of the officers through the events of the past few days. They were in the kitchen, where Charlotte had provided blankets and hot chocolate for everyone.

"Pritchard was supposed to be under surveillance," Ned whispered, looking over his shoulder to see whether the officer was paying attention. "But somebody messed up. They said he would have gotten away if it wasn't for you, Hazel. It's like you kind of saved the police!"

"You mean *we* saved them," Hazel said. But she felt a warm glow spread through her insides at the praise.

Ned gave her a small smile.

Hazel looked at her brother, then at Oliver. They

were both pale and drawn; Ned's hands were scratched and filthy. Had he fallen during his flight through the tunnels to get help for Hazel? She could see dark circles under Oliver's eyes.

"Are you guys okay?" Hazel asked.

Ned nodded. He looked at his cousin.

"We're fine. And our stink bombs sure turned out to be pretty powerful weapons, right, Oliver?"

Hazel grinned. "They were brutal. And that was a great throw, Ned—your timing was perfect."

Ned shrugged, but Hazel could tell he was pleased. He punched her lightly on the shoulder. "Yeah, well, it's good you didn't drown. We make a pretty decent team."

Hazel shivered, remembering the chill of the water and the strength of the current.

"Hazel, if you're feeling up to it now, the detectives would like a word with you," a police officer said.

Moments later, an older woman walked in, followed by an elderly man with a gray beard. They introduced themselves as Detective Heather Mallard and Sergeant Steve Bridge, from Interpol, and asked to speak to Hazel alone.

"Now Hazel," Detective Mallard said after the room had been emptied. "Tell us how this mess began."

Hazel started with the morning she'd woken up to

find her father gone, and kept going, for what felt like hours. By the time she reached her icy swim, Hazel's voice was giving out.

"That was brilliant, my dear," the detective said. The sergeant nodded.

"Look, you need to get some sleep now," Detective Mallard was saying. "But since you've answered all our questions, are there any we can answer for you?"

Hazel tried to concentrate. Detective Mallard was giving her a gift, and she didn't want to squander it. Her father! These officers were from Interpol—surely they could help.

"Why is my father in jail?" Hazel asked. "And when is he getting out?"

"It is official police business, of course," Sergeant Bridge said, smoothing his beard.

"Oh, for crying out loud, Steve, after everything this girl and her family have been through," Detective Mallard began, her voice exasperated.

"I'm just saying . . . ," the older man said. But he smiled and shrugged, waiting for his partner to continue.

"Your father has been working as a consultant to Interpol, investigating certain art thefts and forgeries," Detective Mallard explained. "Mostly helping an old friend of his on the force—that Inspector O'Toole, whose email you stumbled upon but didn't read."

Hazel nodded. If only she *had* read that email, maybe a lot of the summer's mysteries would have been solved right then.

"So how does a consultant end up in prison?" Hazel asked. "Did my dad do something wrong?"

"Oh, no," Detective Mallard said. "He went into that prison as part of an undercover operation, pretending to be a crooked art collector and criminal associate of Clive Pritchard. Inspector O'Toole was going to use a police officer for the job, but at the last minute the fellow became very ill; your father offered to fill in for him."

"Did it work?" Hazel asked.

"I'm told your father has succeeded beyond our wildest expectations."

"You don't sound too happy about it," Hazel remarked.

"Oh, I am; I mean, we are," the detective said. "But there was a mix-up and—I'm very sorry about this—your father has ended up spending considerably more time behind bars than anyone planned."

"What do you mean?" Hazel asked. "What kind of mix-up?"

"Inspector O'Toole was the one running the operation in Istanbul," Sergeant Bridge explained. "But she was hit by a car just after the Turkish police put your father in jail. She's all right now. But for a while nobody was monitoring your father's situation."

When she saw the look on Hazel's face, the detective rushed in. "Your father is fine, I promise. Still, it was a very regrettable mix-up."

"You can say that again." It was Ned. He and Oliver and the twins had entered without Hazel noticing.

"So our dad's out of jail now? He's coming home?" Ned asked.

"Yes, he's out of jail." Sergeant Bridge nodded. "It will be a few days before he can actually return home, though. There's a great deal of paperwork to complete, and the Turkish authorities need to conduct their own inquiry."

Hazel didn't feel reassured. What kind of police force gets someone's dad to do them a favor and then forgets about him *while he's in jail*?

"One thing I don't understand," Mark said, and Hazel could tell he was still angry too, "is how Hazel ended up with one of Pritchard's fakes."

"Oh yes—we'll be taking that with us," Sergeant Bridge said. "Evidence, I'm afraid."

"That's okay—I know my dad meant to give me a different painting," Hazel said. "But how did they get switched?"

"Just before he left for Europe, your father posed as an interested buyer for a Cafazzo," Detective Mallard said. "Inspector O'Toole asked him to bring the Cafazzo, but it seems he just grabbed the wrong painting on the way out."

"So when did he realize that I had a Cafazzo painting?" Hazel asked.

"He didn't—not until your uncle got to Istanbul and told him about it," Sergeant Bridge said. Detective Mallard nodded.

"We *thought* it was a Cafazzo," Ned said. "And we were confused, because it looks so much like this castle."

"It does," Sergeant Bridge agreed. "Almost all of the Cafazzo paintings do. Clive Pritchard seems to have been obsessed with Land's End."

"Look, we'd like to talk more, but I'm afraid the sergeant and I really need to speak with some of the officers," Detective Mallard said. "Thank you for your patience, all of you. And try not to look so glum. You've done good work here, and we're all very grateful."

As the screen door swung closed behind the pair, Ned muttered something under his breath. Hazel didn't catch the words, but the tone was far from pleasant.

"Look, kids, I'm starving." Charlotte glanced at her watch. "We won't be able to rest until all the cops and robbers have cleared out, so we might as well eat."

Nobody would let Hazel help, not even to set the table. She sat back in the chair and watched as everyone else bustled around the room. Ned and Oliver had obviously showered and changed their clothes while she was talking with the detectives. They looked wide-awake, too. Hazel closed her eyes. When she opened them again, Deirdre was tugging on her arm and gesturing toward the table, which was now laden with food.

"I can't believe Dad was working as some kind of undercover agent all along," Ned said between mouthfuls of scrambled egg, bacon, toast, and jam.

"*Almost* all along," corrected Mark as he set one last platter of bacon and sausage on the kitchen table. "It sounds like it got a little too real toward the end, when this O'Toole person dropped out of the picture, and nobody in Istanbul knew Uncle Colin was just pretending to be a criminal."

"Well, I think he could have at least told *us*," Ned said, jabbing at a sausage. "I mean, we could have kept his secret. And after all, it was my project that tipped him off about Clive Pritchard being Paolo Cafazzo."

"This family has a long history of secrets," Oliver said disapprovingly.

A silence descended on the table then, and everyone concentrated on eating. After at least ten minutes, Hazel put down her fork and pushed her plate away with a sigh of satisfaction.

"That was great," she told Mark. "I had no idea how hungry I was."

"If you're anything like me, you felt like you hadn't eaten in about eighteen hours," Mark said, "which is exactly how long it *has* been since we ate a real meal."

"I'm going to go check on the cops," Matt said, pushing back his chair.

"I'll come with you," Deirdre said.

Hazel didn't know where they found the energy to care what the police were doing. She laid her head on the table and closed her eyes again. After a few minutes, though, she opened them.

"Hey—what day is it?" she asked no one in particular.

"It's Monday," Charlotte informed her as the screen door slammed.

Matt strode in, Deirdre at his heels. "Come outside!" he said. "Now!"

"Why?" asked Oliver, shoveling one last forkful of egg into his mouth as he spoke. "Whassup?"

"They're taking them off the island," said Deirdre excitedly. "Clive Pritchard and Kenny Pritchard's father and Paul Fazza. They're taking them to the jail in Frontenac."

"And they're bringing them *here* first?" Hazel asked. She felt a queasy sensation that had nothing to do with the meal she'd just wolfed down. "No thanks. I don't think I want to get that close to those guys again."

"No, they're not coming here," Matt said. "They're taking them to Frontenac by boat. They'll be sailing past any second now."

"We thought we should see them go," Deirdre said. "All of us together, you know, like an honor guard—except, I guess, more of a *dis*honor guard."

"Come on, Hazel, all for one and one for all," Mark said, holding out his hand. "They can't hurt you now."

Hazel nodded reluctantly.

As the children hurried toward the pebbly shore, they passed one of the officers. "Come to see them being taken away?" he asked Hazel. "You should feel proud of what you've done. I hear they've ripped off thousands of people over the years."

"We are proud," said Hazel, linking arms with Ned and Oliver. "The whole team."

"Hmm . . . yeah, I heard about those bombs. You kids want to make sure you use your powers for good, not evil, right?" the officer said, giving the boys a stern look.

"We promise," Oliver said solemnly. Ned nodded.

"Off you go then—you don't want to miss the show." The officer broke into a friendly grin.

The children fell silent as they reached the shore. The largest of the police boats was just backing away from the island, and they could see many uniformed officers aboard.

"I don't see Pritchard," Ned muttered.

"I do," Deirdre said. "Look—Clive Pritchard and Kenny's dad. They're sitting in the stern. That Fazza guy, he's standing a few feet away."

"Oh, and don't they look cranky," said Mark as the boat swung closer.

It was all Hazel could do not to look away. Paul Fazza shook his fist angrily and shouted words they were relieved they couldn't make out over the roar of the boat's engines. Kenny's father didn't even look up; he was slumped in his seat, his shoulders hunched.

But Clive Pritchard, to Hazel's astonishment, rose to his feet as the boat drew near, and met the gaze of the watching children. As his eyes met Hazel's, he gave a mocking smile and, despite his handcuffs, swept a low, graceful bow.

"Cheeky beggar," said a voice behind Hazel. Turning to look, Hazel realized the Frumps had been joined by Sergeant Bridge and Detective Mallard, who were looking out at the boat.

"That's for you, you know," Detective Mallard said, nudging Hazel. "Not us."

Confused, Hazel turned back toward the boat. All the officers on board had arrayed themselves in a line, as far away from the handcuffed captives as possible. Every officer had his or her hand raised in a salute.

Hazel stretched, yawned, and stretched again. Sunlight was streaming through the open windows of her tower room, and at least three cardinals in the tree below were vying with each other to see who could sing the loudest. She felt rested, as if she had slept for days. Yet her watch showed it was early in the morning—only six thirty.

Hazel's stomach growled. She shivered as she tossed back the covers. It had been hot and sticky, without a hint of a breeze, when she'd finally been able to crawl into her bed. A cold front must have moved in overnight. She pulled on a sweatshirt and sweatpants over the T-shirt and shorts she'd slept in, then headed for the stairs.

The house was so quiet, she began to wonder if

everyone else had woken up before her and gone out; but as she passed Deirdre's room, she could hear her cousin snoring gustily away. Stifling a grin, Hazel continued down the stairs to the kitchen, hoping to find Mark awake and preparing one of his amazing breakfast feasts. But only Ned was at the table, an empty cereal bowl in front of him.

"Happy birthday," he said.

Hazel poured a glass of juice. "My birthday's tomorrow. But thanks."

Ned smiled wanly. "Nope. Today."

"I think I know when my birthday is," Hazel said, helping herself to a sticky bun.

"Your watch has a thing that tells the date." Ned pointed. "Look at it and you'll see I'm right—it's the day *after* the day that you think it is."

Hazel stared at her watch. Ned was telling the truth; it was Wednesday. No wonder her stomach was growling! Now that she thought about it, her injured wrist wasn't even sore anymore; all the swelling had disappeared. She waggled her fingers: good as new.

"Wow. I've never slept that long in my whole life," she said with a grin.

"More than a whole day," Ned said. "Listen, I did some snooping yesterday, while you were asleep. I found some old letters and some newspaper clippings and . . . well, I found out some weird stuff about our family."

"Like what?"

"For starters, our mother had a sister named Julia, who married Uncle Seamus."

"What?" Hazel stared at Ned. "Seriously?"

Ned nodded, his expression somber. "I guess it's sort of like a fairy tale. You know, two brothers marrying two sisters."

A sudden thought struck Hazel. "Were they twins too—Mom and Julia?"

"No . . ." Ned started polishing his glasses. "It turns out it's not a coincidence that our mom and our aunt both died. They died *together*, Hazel, in a car crash."

Hazel felt her stomach drop. A car crash? Her mother had died in a car crash, and no one had told her, not even her cousins. Hazel stared at her brother, but Ned looked just as confused and unhappy as she felt. Hazel guessed there was more, but Ned didn't seem in a hurry to tell her.

"Anything else?" Hazel said finally, trying not to cry.

"Yeah. For one thing, I found out Charlotte isn't a Frump. She's from our mothers' side of the family. I guess that's why Matt and Mark and Deirdre didn't want to explain how she was related."

Hazel swallowed hard. She hadn't even thought about the family on her mother's side. Were there other cousins? Grandparents?

"Let's go for a walk," Hazel said. "I'd rather not have to see anybody else right now. I need some time to think about all this."

Ned grabbed a Windbreaker from a peg near the door and led the way to the porch. A fresh breeze was blowing off the lake, and the water glinted in the sunshine. As they made their way through the apple orchard to the dunes, Hazel stole a glance at Ned. His face was troubled.

"There really *is* something going on with all the adults this summer," Hazel said. "They just don't seem to stick around."

"Except Charlotte," Ned said. "She told me last night she's not leaving until Uncle Seamus shows up, just in case we decide to have any more adventures."

"Hmm," Hazel replied. "I think I speak for everyone when I say I've had enough adventures to last me a long, long time."

Ned nodded. They had reached the beach, and Hazel still had the impression there was something he wasn't telling her. She watched as Ned selected a flat gray pebble and skipped it across the surface of the lake.

"So all the mysteries have been solved, then," she said.

Ned sent another pebble skipping across the waves. It bounced four times before disappearing from view.

As Hazel watched, he skipped another and then another. Each time, the pebbles bounced effortlessly four times off the water's surface. Hazel wondered how he did that.

"All the mysteries," Hazel repeated. "Well, all but one. We still don't know why Dad kept us away from here all our lives."

Ned launched another pebble over the waves. It sank as soon as it hit the water.

"That mystery's been solved too."

"What?"

"I told you I found some newspaper clippings," Ned began. "I figured out some stuff, and then I went to Charlotte last night, after everyone had gone to bed. I told her she had to tell me the rest."

Hazel waited. She could see that Ned was struggling not to cry. He took a deep breath and continued.

"There was this party in Frontenac. Dad really wanted to go and so did Aunt Julia—Oliver was just a few months old and she hadn't been out much. Mom wasn't big on parties, but she knew they both really wanted her to go. So Uncle Seamus stayed home with all us kids. Charlotte—she was a teenager back then—came over to help babysit. And Mom and Dad and Aunt Julia drove to the ferry."

"Only they never made it?" Hazel asked.

Ned winced.

"There used to be this really bad stretch of road on the island," he said. "The driver lost control, and the car went off the road and Mom and her sister were killed instantly."

Hazel's heart was pounding now.

"Who was driving?" she asked. But even before the answer came, she knew.

"Dad."

Hazel couldn't speak. A tear slipped down her cheek. Then another.

"They said there was nothing he could have done," Ned said. "There was even an inquest and everything, and everybody agreed it wasn't his fault. Afterward, it came out that some people on the town council—including Kenny Pritchard's dad—had been warned the road was really dangerous. They were supposed to have fixed it, but they hadn't. They fixed it later, of course."

Of course. Hazel was silent for a few moments, watching the waves rise and fall. Colin Frump didn't own a car now. She had never seen him drive. She had thought he didn't know how.

"I guess Uncle Seamus and the cousins," she began, "I guess they were pretty mad at Dad. I mean, I guess *they* blamed him, even if nobody else did."

"I don't know," Ned said.

"But Dad knew, because he kept us apart," Hazel

said. "He blamed himself. He knew they blamed him."

"You don't know that," Ned said. "Anyway, maybe they *were* angry back then, but they're not now. You can tell. If we ask them, I'm sure they'll say so."

But Hazel wasn't listening. She was picturing their father at the scene of the crash. Had he been injured too? Did he try to go for help?

Hazel felt sick to her stomach. When someone dies instantly, is it really instant, she wondered? Did her aunt have time to realize she was dying and know that she would never see her baby again? Did her mother call out for her or Ned?

"They all would have hated him," she said quietly. "And he knew they'd end up hating us, too, because our father killed their mother."

Hazel had been sitting on the soft dunes, hugging her knees to her chest and staring out across the lake. Now she reached over and pulled her brother down beside her. It was as if the world had been turned inside out. She didn't want to believe in something so horrible. She wanted to tell Ned to take it back, to admit he'd made it all up.

But it had to be true. It explained so much, like why her father never talked about their mother and why none of the cousins would tell her the reason the families had kept apart for so long.

Ned was crying quietly. Hazel wrapped her arms around him and held him tight. She was too shocked to cry. Too angry. How could her father have kept something like this from them? It was the same thing as a lie. She found herself miserably reliving every conversation she'd ever had with Colin Frump about their family or her mother, and sorrow mixed with her anger. Her father must have felt so guilty. So what if it wasn't his fault? Hazel knew Colin Frump. She knew he blamed himself. What had he said to her, as they stood on the cliff? *The fear is not that you will fall, but that you will jump?* He must have spent years replaying the crash over and over, wondering if he could have done something differently. One tiny little thing, maybe. And then six children wouldn't have had to grow up without their mothers, and two men wouldn't have had to raise their families alone.

No wonder Dad had never brought them back here.

When the tears finally came, it was a relief. Hazel wept for what seemed a very long time. When she finally ran out of tears, it took her a moment to realize Ned had stopped too. Her face was swollen and she desperately needed to blow her nose. Ned found some Kleenex in the pocket of his jacket, and they blew their noses and wiped their eyes.

"I really think Uncle Seamus and the cousins aren't

angry at Dad now," Ned said. "Or they wouldn't have tried so hard to help him."

The fresh breeze had turned into a wind, and seagulls keened overhead. Hazel stood up and stretched out a hand.

"This is a birthday I'm never going to forget. Come on, Squirt—let's go face the others."

But it wasn't as hard as Hazel had expected. Charlotte and the cousins were waiting for them when they entered the kitchen, and from the looks on everyone's faces, it was clear they had guessed why Ned and Hazel had wanted to be alone. There were more hugs and tears all around, but once it had been established that the truth was finally out and nobody blamed anyone for anything, Charlotte took charge.

"Time for you to have hot showers and get dressed so we get on with birthday celebrations," she said, shooing them out of the kitchen.

It was a birthday unlike any other. After lunch, Mark produced the strangest cake Hazel had ever seen. Iced in a garish orange frosting, it was in the shape of a basketball. But not half a basketball, with the rounded side facing up. Somehow they had fashioned a cake just as round and wobbly as an actual basketball.

The cousins presented Hazel with a hoard of presents, including an enormous crate that turned out to contain an NBA regulation-size basketball hoop. The birthday was complete.

And that night, the Frumps dragged out all their old family photo albums, and Hazel and Ned were given lengthy histories for everyone from distant cousins to great-grandparents. The reason for Ned and Oliver's close resemblance was explained when Hazel found a faded photograph of the maternal grandfather they shared: He was a short, slender man with straight brown hair and dark eyes partly obscured by a pair of spectacles. In the picture he was standing proudly beside a bizarre contraption, which resembled a hang glider that had sprouted hundreds of tiny propellers.

"Mom used to tell us her father was always inventing something," Matt told Ned, "including his own versions of what he called personal aircraft. Some of them actually flew, although not very far."

Hazel didn't like the gleam of approval she detected in Ned's eyes as he studied the photograph. But her attention was distracted by the appearance of an album overflowing with pictures of her mother. To Hazel's delight, the smiling woman in the photographs had the same green eyes and pale, freckled skin that she had. In fact, all the features of her face bore a remarkable resemblance to Hazel's. But where Hazel was tall and long limbed, her mother was petite, like

Ned and Oliver. Worse, her mother's long, thick hair was as sandy in color as Deirdre's short mop. Hazel couldn't hide her disappointment.

"But you still do look a lot like Aunt Jane," Deirdre said comfortingly. "If you ask me, you look more like your mother than I look like mine."

"Really?" Hazel replied.

Deirdre grinned. "Let me show you what I mean," she said, pulling another album from the shelf. "Check out *my* mother."

Aunt Julia's face, smiling out at Hazel from the photographs, actually did look a little like Deirdre, Hazel reflected. However, her rangy frame was a perfect match for Hazel's, and her unkempt mane of hair was every bit as red.

"Wow," Ned observed, peering over Hazel's shoulder. "You're like a total blend of the two sisters. It's like there isn't a speck of DNA from Dad's side of the family."

"I look just like my mother, too," Mark said.

"How do you know?" Ned asked.

"Our mother died when we were six," Matt said quietly. "It was cancer. But she had known for a long time that the treatments weren't working, and since she was closer to your uncle Seamus and aunt Julia than she was to her own family, she asked them to become our guardians."

Hazel's eyes widened in shock. Her mind was quickly doing the math, but Mark got there before she could.

"Yup. That means we lost our first mother when we were six, and our second mother—your aunt—when we were nine," he said.

"Oh boy," Ned said, shaking his head.

"No wonder our dad couldn't face you," Hazel whispered.

"Hey, that's enough of that," Matt said. "We're not going to deny that it was rough. We still miss both of them—and Aunt Jane too, for that matter. But I thought we all agreed that it was time to move on."

"The accident really wasn't Uncle Colin's fault," Mark added. "We know that, Hazel. Maybe that was hard for us to grasp eight years ago, but we realize it now."

"You should know that our dad sat down with us a few years ago and went through all the newspaper clippings and the coroner's report, just to make sure we really did understand," Matt said. "We've had a long time to come to grips with it. It must be hard for you and Ned, getting hit with everything all at once."

"But you *have* to deal with it," Deirdre said. "So that when Uncle Colin gets here, you can help him. Because if you ask me, it's time we all stopped letting the past control the present. We're a family again, and that's how it's going to stay!"

Deirdre's words reverberated in Hazel's head as she climbed into bed that night. They *were* a family. They were a terrific family. So why was it that, for the first time in years, Hazel found herself missing her mother? Tears pricked at her eyelids. If only her mother were here, maybe she could help Colin Frump deal with the past. Hazel sighed. That made no sense. If her mother *were* here, there would be no past for her father to deal with. There was no sense wishing things were different.

"I'll just have to help Dad myself," Hazel said aloud into the quiet of her darkened tower room.

20

Hazel opened her eyes. She was in the tower again. She could feel the cool flagstones beneath her cheek. The stars outside the gothic window were shining their cold light over the easels and canvases that filled the round room.

What was she doing here again? It was the dream, she knew that. But she hadn't had the dream in more than a week. She had begun to believe she'd never have it again. Why was she back here, trapped in this room?

"Get up," the woman's voice urged.

"I can't," Hazel replied. Then she realized it wasn't true: She could move. Her legs were no longer paralyzed. She rose.

The tower room was filled with paintings, many of

them unfinished. A long wooden table beside her held an array of paints and brushes, and rags for cleaning the brushes. The waves below the open window pounded against the rocks. She turned to the easel closest to her. It was shrouded in white canvas. Hazel stretched out a trembling hand toward it. She had to see what lay underneath.

"It's time, Hazel," the woman said. *"This is where you are supposed to be."*

"Okay, sure. Just let me look at this," Hazel said.

"Now, Hazel!" the voice insisted. *"It's time. Come!"*

A sudden sense of urgency gripped Hazel, and her hand fell to her side. She *was* needed. Now.

"I'm coming!" Hazel called out, and her eyes flew open.

She bolted out of bed. It was early. Outside her window, dawn had broken, but the daylight was still weak. The only sounds were those of birds trilling in the treetops, but Hazel could still hear her own name ringing in her ears. She had to go.

Hazel threw open her door and flew down the stairs. She raced silently along the corridors, her heartbeat almost drowning out the voice that echoed in her head. Hazel knew where she had to go, and she wasn't the least bit afraid this time. When she came to the cellar and the entrance to the tunnels, she hardly paused to let her eyes adjust to the dark. She just kept running.

The heavy oak door that connected the tunnels to the tower was standing open. Hazel hesitated, but nine days after her escape from Clive Pritchard, there was no longer even a trace of the stink bomb. Hazel climbed the steep stairs to the trapdoor and heaved it up, entering the empty ground-floor room slightly out of breath. Her eyes were fixed on the curving stone staircase. The trapdoor at the top, leading to the upper story, was open.

Hazel's fear of heights checked her stride for a fraction of a second before she began climbing. The sense of urgency she'd felt in the dream had not ebbed. She could still hear the voice in her head, insisting she come.

As Hazel climbed toward the opening, her ears strained, but all she could hear were the waves outside. When at last she pulled herself into the room at the top of the Martello tower, she was startled to find it almost empty. There were no easels, no brushes and paints. But Hazel knew she had finally returned to the tower of her dream. The long wooden table was still there, near the tall arched window. And standing behind the table, with his back to Hazel, a man was gazing out that window.

"Dad?" Hazel whispered. "Daddy?"

The tall, dark-haired man turned at the sound of

her voice, just in time to be nearly knocked over as Hazel rushed into his arms.

"Hazel?" her father said, lifting her off the ground. "Why aren't you still in bed? How did you get here? And how did you know I was here?"

Colin Frump stepped back to look into his daughter's face, but held fast to her shoulders as if he couldn't risk letting go.

"I don't know, I just—I had this dream and I had to come," Hazel said. She was laughing and crying at the same time. "How did you get here?"

"Frankie and Seamus and I flew back together last night," her father replied. "We took Frankie home first, and drove through the night. I thought it would be hours before any of you woke up. So I figured I would just . . . come here."

He broke off, looking around the deserted room.

"Do you remember this place, Hazel?" he asked. The words sounded as though they hurt him.

"Just from my dreams," Hazel replied.

"Your dreams?" her father repeated. He frowned.

"Yes. I've dreamed about this room for years," Hazel said. "What is this place, Daddy? And why did you come here?"

"This was your mother's studio," her father said. "She loved the light in this room. I haven't been here since . . ."

"Since when?" prompted Hazel.

"I haven't been here since the day of the accident," her father answered, squaring his shoulders. "I gather you know all about that now."

"Yes," Hazel said. Her chin wobbled slightly, but she kept her voice steady. "Everybody knows. And everybody knows it wasn't your fault. And everybody agrees it's time you came home and we all started being a family again."

Her dad swallowed. "I'm proud of you and your brother, you know. Figuring out what Clive Pritchard was up to . . . although I suppose I should be grounding you or something for putting yourselves at risk the way you did. . . ."

"Dad. Don't change the subject," Hazel began, but her father held up a hand to silence her.

"I'm not changing the subject," he said heavily. "I was going to say that as grateful as I am for your detecting skills, I am even more grateful that you managed to bring our family back together."

Hazel could see that her father was struggling not to cry. She could feel a tingling in her nose warning her that her own tears weren't far off.

"Well, as long as you're not mad about missing a great birthday party," Hazel tried to joke.

Her father took a deep breath. "Yes, I'm sorry about that too. And I understand that you received the wrong painting for a present. I have with me here the painting I intended you to have. . . ."

He turned away from Hazel, and she saw a small, flat package wrapped in brown paper leaning against the wall behind him. He placed it on the wooden table and began slowly unwrapping it.

"You may have been too young at the time to remember this," he said. "But I've been keeping it for you. I wanted to wait until you were ready . . . or perhaps, if I'm honest, until I was ready. Do you remember this?"

Hazel stared. Her father was holding a family portrait that showed Hazel as a little girl, her arms wrapped around a baby, who was clearly Ned. Both he and Hazel were laughing, their faces turned toward a younger, happier-looking image of their father. A smiling woman was holding his hand. Even without the photographs she had seen the night before, Hazel would have known it was her mother.

"You used to come here all the time to watch Janey work," her father said, staring at the canvas. "She would give you finger paints, watercolors, markers— anything you liked. The two of you spent hours in this room."

"I *remember* this painting," Hazel said. She could hardly breathe.

"Your mother was working on it the day she died.

She'd promised you she would finish it that day, but I made her come with me and Julia to that stupid party. You were upset; she had said she'd give you the painting to hang in your room when it was done. So she promised you that no matter how late we stayed out, when she got back, she would come straight here and finish it.

"That night—the night of the accident—you must have crept out of bed after Seamus had tucked you in, and come back here to wait for her. How you managed it on your own, through all those dark tunnels . . . I wondered about that for years. Anyway, somehow you found your way here, and you waited all night. When I came home from the hospital, I found the entire household in an uproar. First, of course, because of the accident. But then because nobody could find you."

"Who found me?" Hazel whispered.

"I did. You were curled up on the floor right over there, beside your mother's easel."

Hazel slipped her arm around her father's waist and stared at the painting. She felt sad for the little girl who had waited by herself, all night long, for a mother who would never come. But she didn't remember that night, not really, just the dream version.

Still—and this was odd—she remembered the painting. She remembered how happy everyone looked.

As Hazel thought about how her mother had wanted to give the painting to her, the craziest idea came to her. That voice in her dreams . . . could it have been her mother's?

Hazel opened her mouth to tell her father and then closed it again. This was the sort of secret it was okay to keep. But right now, he needed her help with one last thing.

"Are you hungry?" she asked her father. "Because I am. And you probably don't know this, but they make a pretty decent breakfast here."

Her dad laughed. It was a little nervous, Hazel decided, but it wasn't an unhappy laugh.

"I don't know if I'm ready to see everybody just yet," her father began.

"Well, you don't have much of a choice, because they're ready to see you," Hazel told him, pushing him toward the trapdoor. "Only we better stop by Ned's room before we hit the kitchen. He'll flip when he finds out I saw you first."

As the two of them made their way down the stairs, Hazel squeezed her father's hand.

"I'm glad you're back," she told him.

"So am I," said her father.

ACKNOWLEDGMENTS

Jane Lanthier (1942–2006) read every version except this last one. This book would not have been written without her support and that of Stephen Rogers, Nicola, Buzz, and James Lanthier-Rogers. This book would not have been published without the efforts of Nina Richmond, Lynne Missen, and Akka Janssen. When I was tempted to give up, Ginger Knowlton, Barbara Berson, and the brilliant Heather Mallick encouraged me to continue. The talents of Sheryl Barton, Karen Jordan, Nanci Kirkland, and Andrea Steele made it possible for me to write and edit. Kelci Gershon gave me a key and a place to work. Carol Jupiter, Carolyn Kennedy, Jane Crist, Nicky Lanthier-Rogers, Kelsey McDougall, Cameron Scrivens, Karen Jordan, and Richard Scrimger read various versions and gave invaluable advice. Mary-Ann Roberts and her class of 2004/2005 were insightful and inspiring and earned my thanks forever. Thanks are also due to Noelle Zitzer, Lina Loparco, Natasha Daneman, and Jill Goodman. I needed all the help I could get from the basketball gurus: James Lanthier, Nicky Lanthier-Rogers, Nancy, Margot, and Jill Eisenhauer. For their patience and professionalism, I am indebted to Chuck Swirsky and Kevin DiPietro of the Toronto Raptors, Paul Jones and Eric Smith, Jillian Svensson of Maple Leaf Sports and Entertainment, and Tanya Phillipps of Canada Basketball. Sheelagh Frame, Sadie Frame, Victoria Gall, Maxine Hersch, and The Runners (Julie Cohen, Paige Cowan, Claire Cram, Gillian Cummings, Janet Deacon, Susan Doyle, Ruth Durgy, Chris Filipiuk, Heather Gardiner, Susan Gordon, Julia Holland, Katherine Lake Berz, Michelle Martin, Carrie Scace, and Carol Wildi) always had my back. Andrée-Anne Gagnon, Cybèle Lanthier, Louise Setlakwe, and Julia Holland are not responsible for any errors I may have made on behalf of Monsieur Gentil. I would also like to thank Suzanne Baby and the Hart House Gallery Grill, E. Nesbit, Joss Whedon, Berry, Buck, Mills, and Stipe, and of course, Jill Santopolo, who worked tirelessly and brilliantly on the final draft of this book. Final thanks must go to the young Alvin Williams, #20 forever—may his daughter always have a basketball in her hands.